Charlotte Emma Gledson

Black Hound Presents

THE LONELY TREE AND OTHER TWISTED TALES OF TORMENT

By

Charlotte Emma Gledson

Horror that is close to home

Charlotte Emma Gledson

THE LONELY TREE

AND OTHER

TWISTED TALES OF TORMENT

By

Charlotte Emma Gledson

Charlotte Emma Gledson

THE LONELY TREE AND OTHER TWISTED TALES OF TORMENT

Copyright Notice: by Charlotte Emma Gledson.

All rights reserved.

The above information forms this copyright notice: © *2008 by Charlotte Emma Gledson. All rights reserved.*

No part of this publication can be distributed by any means without prior, written consent from the copyright owner.

Edited by Jordan M Bobé

Cover art designed by Doodlemonkie.

© 2008 by Doodlemonkie. For further information about the artist go to www.doodlemonkie.com

This is a work of fiction. All of the characters, names, incidents, organisations and dialogue is the product of the author's imagination, and is used fictitiously.

Published by Black Hound

ISBN:978-0-9559778-0-0

Printed in the United Kingdom

This book is dedicated to Liza Virgina Winkfield Rutter and her brood of adorable golden angels; Chloe Elizabeth, Jessica Rose, Lucy Eleanor and Sarah Lilly Langford Rutter.

Also to my husband John Gledson, who has made a difference to my life. I want to thank you for being you, never change.

I dedicate this book to my children, Samuel John, William Thomas, Daniel Adam, Bethany Emma Maureen and Edward Matthew Gledson. All of you are so different and such characters please stay unique.

Finally this book is for my father, John Gradon; the lonely man that loved deeply, but could only express this through the written word, music and through nature's wonder.

Charlotte Emma Gledson

THE LONELY TREE AND OTHER TWISTED TALES OF TORMENT

PREFACE	10
ACKNOWLEDGEMENTS	12
INTRODUCTION BY JORDAN M. BOBÈ	15
THE LONELY TREE	17
THE BOYS' NIGHT OUT	25
SHALLOW CRIES	30
IT'S A DOG'S LIFE	39
THE CHRISTMAS CURSE	48
THE HAND THAT FEEDS	52
GROWING PAINS	61
TO HAVE AND TO HOLD	64
DON'T LOOK DOWN	76
FIRST IMPRESSION	79
THE LETTER	91
A TASTE OF YOUR OWN MEDICINE	99
SHADOW MAN	112
PARANOIA	125
PRESENCE	127
TOOLS	133
THE ROUND WINDOW	134
CHECKING OUT	149
RETRIBUTION	159
PRAISE FOR CHARLOTTE EMMA GLEDSON	168
ABOUT THE AUTHOR	170

PREFACE

Two years ago I had a sudden spark of vision. I was almost reaching forty years of age and I wanted to feel I had achieved something.

A personal creative accolade.

After marrying the man that changed my life considerably after a turbulent and testing past, I eventually began living my life with a new sense of freedom and personal growth. The seed to write finally emerged. I felt compelled to creatively release myself. This man made me laugh again. I 'lived' life for the first time and to be honest, a day does not go by without us having a chuckle in spite of some harrowing times we have faced. I have committed some grave mistakes in the past, but he has always stood by me, protected me and forgiven me. He is my saving grace.

Many ask why I write such psychological, terrifying and indeed explicit material. I simply answer by saying that the evils that exist behind closed doors in our everyday world, encapsulate the truest of horrors. The horrors that lie within ourselves, such as our vices, insecurities and inadequacies, are equally as terrifying. This is what I am trying to illustrate. Sadly for many, however, horrific acts *do* take place which scar and mar the human psyche, leading one onto the road to destruction and affecting those closest to them.

I have four gregarious children, all of whom have made a difference to my life. They reward me with feelings of wellbeing, tenderness and pride. My son Daniel nevertheless, will never be forgotten. He moulded me into the woman I am today. I wrote my first poem for him. This was the pivotal point in my life that urged me to put pen to paper. My need to write finally blossomed. In spite of my Dyslexia and Dyspraxia I never felt the need to abandon my writings; I enjoyed it too much! The fear of the written word was now in *my* control.

As my other children grow and begin to form their own identities and relationships, I felt it was the right time to record my fears, express hidden feelings and unburden my heavy mind. So I started to write a collection of poems called 'Turbulent Emotions'. Then the short stories oozed out of me, thanks to my dear friends I met on Myspace. I found a huge surge of therapeutic relief once I penned my feelings. The power of the pen is indeed mightier than the sword!

My father loved to read and listen to classical music. I recall him telling me as a child his love for ghost stories such as M.R. James's '*Oh whistle, and I will come to you, my lad.*' He would tell me about his love of Poe and as an impressionable teen, I dwelled on his every word. He started reading me a story that he created about a sinister character called '*Nabob*' and this character fascinated me. My father died soon after. Still to this day, the moments we shared talking about ghost stories, his love for steam trains, gardening and bird song are the only times I saw him happy, animated and excited. He also had written a few poems that evoked emotion within me, echoing his own regret that he never did achieve his own personal dream. He wanted so much to write, just like his father.

So, here I am. I am writing because my father would be proud of me and *his* talent lies within me.

Thank you.

ACKNOWLEDGEMENTS

Most sincerely I would like to thank all those at Word Weavers, who had faith in me from the very start!

Also to Jordan M. Bobé for publishing my first story *Presence*, in the Darkened Horizons horror/macabre anthologies.

Personal friendships and support from other esteemed authors that believed in me are; Matthew Alan Pierce, Jeff Ezell, Ben Eads, Jessica Lynne Gardner, Jeanna Tendean, Cassandra Lee and Andrew Wolter.

My special thanks go to Doodlemonkie for doing the excellent cover art. He has helped me enormously. Find his work at www.doodlemonkie.com.

Ultimately the support comes from my family. My sister Liza Rutter; who has patiently proof read all my twisted tales and encouraged me ten fold. At the drop of hat, she would listen to my ramblings over the phone. And to my husband John Gledson, who helped edited and critiqued all my stories. He taught me all I know. Also to my aunt, Keri Spencer, who indeed gave me that extra push of encouragement that I so needed.

Finally I thank all my children, Sam, Billy, Bethany and Eddy for being so patient and undemanding when I am writing, allowing me the space and time

I need to complete a story. My mother in law Maureen, although her first love is not horror, has never lost faith.

And finally my mother, I thank you too…

Note: *The Lonely Tree* and *The Hand That Feeds* first appeared in Ladies of Horror 2008 from Word Weavers Press.

A taste of your own medicine first appeared in Word Weavers Requiem for the Damned.

Presence, Shallow Cries, Retribution, To Have and to Hold and *Retribution* first appeared in Darkened Horizons Horror Anthologies, edited by Jordan M Bobé

Charlotte Emma Gledson

INTRODUCTION BY JORDAN M. BOBÉ

Reading Charlotte Emma Gledson can prove to be rather dangerous. Her stories of incredible human evil may make you look a little closer at your neighbours. What Stephen King did for Maine Gledson does for the UK. I, for one, do not want to go on vacation anywhere near the people she describes.

Charlotte's skills as a writer originate from poetry, which is obvious with her lyrical prose. No matter what diabolical evil she is describing, Charlotte manages to bring a beauty to her words. No one writes horror like Gledson.

Though her stories primarily focus on human evil there are no two stories that are similar. Every character that she creates is unique. The power behind her stories lies within the people that she creates. They are beautiful, they are disgusting, they are happy, they are terrifying, but above all else they are all *human*.

The world is a dark, foreboding place and Gledson knows it. Take her hand and walk through the darkness so that, perhaps, you will survive the attack when your friendly neighbour turns into a sociopathic, homicidal maniac.

The Lonely Tree has an array of stories. No matter how much you like or dislike horror you will find something within the pages that will make you love Mrs. Gledson. The stories are dark, terrifying and often sad. You will never find a collection quite like this one. And you will never find an author quite like Charlotte. - **Jordan M Bobé, editor of the *Darkened Horizons Anthologies* and author of *The Retreat*.**

Charlotte Emma Gledson

THE LONELY TREE

The mist crept over the estuary, gliding its moist cloud over the sandy banks of the slivery streaked water. I walked down the sodden loam that hugged the pure green fertile fields. A cacophony of urgent chatter from neighbouring magpies and roosting rooks broke the radiant silence as I was wandered wearily across the sea of multicoloured fields. These were indeed so flawless; you could visualise a blanket that was embroidered to perfection, causing a myriad of textures; the natural intimate precision being its ultimate unique essence.

Warm wisps of vapour from the sun swelled and dispersed beneath a depressive cloud filling me with an element of hope, completion. This was the distraction I needed as I fled from my home that nestled between a primrose hill and undulating arable pastures. My home harboured tensions and chaos that I could no longer endure. These thoughts consumed me vigorously as I strode down the muddy countryside. I had to escape the clawing restraints of the constant abuse and instability that engulfed my life.

Tractor tracks were carved into the innocent beauty of the immaculate fabric of nature's creation, spewing out the mud spattered dirt, as I sloshed and slipped across the vast meadow. My destination was a tree. It beckoned me. The beguiling branches lured me to its core, willing me to touch the hard jagged rasping bark. I approached the tree that now was silhouetted in front of the rising sun, darkening all colour that was etched on the vast gnarled haphazard branches. No leaves flourished on these sinister barren arms that arched and pleaded out to the mottled heavens, as though offering the dappled sky a wish it could never receive. An empty invitation, yet it held such rich promises.

Under the heavy flaky bole, a red ribbon was caught on a twisted root. Waving acrobatically, it shifted in the brisk wind. The contrast of vivid colour caught my eye as I escaped the discord that filled my home, flooded my life.

Finally I reached the tree. Here I sat underneath its shrouding branches in awe. So expansive were the parasol of twisted fingers, I felt its calming rapture. The stress from my previous hours gradually diminished. I reached for the ribbon. Putting it to my nose I inhaled deeply. Closing my eyes I pictured a blonde girl playing her cello with a looming grand piano behind her. I opened my eyes, dazzled by the stark light. How long had I held my eyes so tightly shut? I felt as though time had stood still. Oh, how I treasured that feeling.

I pulled a stray strand of flaxen hair that was caught within the knot that had been tightly pulled by some invisible hands. Holding the ribbon securely in my fingers, I sat down crossing my legs.

I sat in pensive silence.

Feeling a sense of resolution fill my soul; a flood of conclusion filtered my heart, my mind. I knew what I had to do. I turned and stroked the trunk of the tree rhythmically. Sharp serrated pieces of bark crumbled as I caressed the rippling bole, leaving my palms chaffed and red, but the exquisite pain engrossed me.

A caw from an onlooker broke my hypnotic trance, alerting me that there was indeed urgent work to be done. I turned from my beautiful tree that radiated such warmth. A glow penetrated through my being as the morning sun flourishes a young tender bud. It was time for me to go. I turned away from my safe dwelling and with ribbon in hand; I walked back to the house that had caused me so many sorrows.

***

With joy in my heart contradictory with the now darkening skies above me, I skipped back through the fields. Mud splashed behind me as I jaunted enthusiastically back to the house.

The House.

Yes, it did leave a bitter taste in my mouth, as I knew the reality that lay behind the walls of this quaint charming cottage. Two yew trees graced either side of this building, with a brick well adjacent to the back door. A bridle of rose-hip crawled around the front door, framing the entrance with buds of scarlet, radiating a welcoming scent with a vision of natural beauty.

How charming. How *terrifying*.

My stomach flipped up and over with every nearing step as I approached my home. I passed the graveyard, adorned with an abundance of pink blossom amidst the dreary lichen covered tomb stones.

Breathtakingly beautiful, but painfully scarring. Hurt and menace dwelled within these walls, yet today - though I felt the familiar sting of nerves and apprehension - I sang to myself as I let myself in.

She was in the kitchen, chopping mushrooms aggressively. Her face clouded in the throes of alcohol, turbulent blackness sweeping across her brow as she sustained her brutal hacking. The mushrooms scattered across the work surface.

With the sun cushioned behind a leaden sky she scowled as a mushroom fell to the floor. With an awkward stagger, she leaned over to retrieve the wanton vegetable. As she began to search for the mushroom, I grabbed the inviting knife that was perched on the work counter. I then rammed the silver stark blade in between her shoulder blades; a feeling of complete retribution swamped me. I shrieked at the top of my voice, "*I HATE YOU*" as I twisted the blade into her back, muscle and flesh spiralled against the blade.

With each stab I recalled her hateful deeds. The abuse, the beatings and her ugliness that accompanied her drunken rages, infected my mind.

Oh how I drenched myself in her warm blood. Purposely I layered myself in her hot ruby liquid, by stabbing harder, deeper. Penetrating her spine, I felt my blade scrape the marrow of her bone. I felt completely liberated.

Awash in her blood, I finally dropped the knife. Looking down at her exposed back, I knelt down and turned her hulky weight over. Her eyes were still looking at me. Even in death she was accusing me.

"What I have done?"

This time as I uttered these words, it was not in fear or anxiety. These words came from the serendipity of chance. Yesterday I was a terrified teenager; today I had killed the dragon. I had accomplished something for the first time in my life. The constant belittling was now a faint stain, no longer a black cloak of inadequacy. I felt I had achieved the highest accolade. Yesterday I was losing; today I had won the hardest battle of all. With fleeting feelings of respect, I actually felt I *liked* myself for the very first time.

As her empty gaze continued to judge me, I jabbed my finger into her puffy eye. I felt the slimy membrane pop under the stress as my digit delved into her socket.

"Don't look at me that way, I did nothing wrong. I am a good girl. I try so hard to please you but you still condemn me."

Picking up the knife one more time, I jarred the blade into her ribcage, slicing her upper chest. Here I eventually found the trophy. Scooping up the limp warm heart I placed it into the pocket of my pinafore, alongside the silky ribbon. Together they cuddled up in the recesses of my patchwork pouch.

A strange notion then enveloped me. The woman's heart pulsed with blissful life only minutes before, and now it was nothing more than a wet lump of useless muscle. The denim smock had now lost its royal blue appearance. Scarlet blood coated my wet dripping clothes staining the cloth black.

Finally leaving her gin bloated corpse, I picked up the stray mushroom that she had so fruitlessly tried to salvage and wedged it down her tight throat. I wanted no more slurred insults from her…

Turning from the kitchen that was now a canvas of claret, I left the superficial shallow beauty of my charming home, knowing the real beauty came from only within one's honest heart.

***

Waltzing past the churchyard, crossing the bridge where the shimmering water gushed below, I eventually saw my tree. I felt the urge to return to the place where I had *found myself*. The rook still balanced on the edge of a brittle empty branch. No sun surrounded my tree this time. The sky was shadowy, haunting. I felt the familiar creep of foreboding as I approached its sheltering frame.

Anger stabbed at me as I slumped to the trunk. I didn't want to feel fear again; I had only just eradicated it. Using my bare hands, I began to burrow. I explored and dug the rich ground, breaking my nails in doing so. I eventually made a significant dent into the grassy soil, as an irritated worm squirmed out from beneath the fractured earth. Picking up the slithering desperate nematode, I threw it behind me. I heard the rook flap down from above to grab his long awaited lunch. A chif-chaf whistled lyrically as I continued to excavate the ground. At last I had the perfect hole.

A perfect grave for the not so perfect heart.

I reached into my blood drenched pocket and carefully placed the insipid organ into the shallow cavity. Looking down at the puce, limp muscle for the last time, I envisaged how it must have beat in unison with every stroke of her leather sandal as she pounded my bare buttocks.

Beat. Beat. Beat. Now it pulsed no more. I was now free.

Concealing the buried heart within the shifted earth I began to replace the hole in frantic haste. I did not want to see this article again. Flattening the soil with the palm of my hand I patted the earth carefully, precisely. As I did so, I felt a sudden surge of warmth. I looked up alarmed. No, the sun had not graced me with its presence as it had done earlier; only a murky purpling veil tinged the darkened skies.

The heat was coming from within the tree itself, the earth below was vibrating. Instinctively I picked out the ribbon that was cradled in my pocket. Though blood stained it still had its glossy touch. Inhaling the coppery fabric once more I realised only then, that this ribbon had once been mine. The last time I had worn this was when I had been ten years old. She had pulled it from my hair so brutally that tufts of my hair were torn from its roots. For many years I dismissed this abuse. I had come to think that this was normality. I waited for the insults, I accepted them. I clenched my teeth as the beatings began; I nursed my ego to a minimum. But after years of constant detriment and humiliation, I had no more self respect to nurse.

Until now.

The heat continued to engulf me, I felt the shuddering persist. The rook finally fled. I started to get up, but I was entrenched to the ground. I felt the rumbling roots wriggle beneath me.

Looking up I could see the tree turning red, scarlet embers glowed from around the whole structure. Still trying desperately hard to flee, sweat poured from my blood-soaked pores as a root began to penetrate me, forcing its thin twisted appendage up into my vagina. The pain consumed me. The channel of my womanhood ripped and tore as flashes of the massacre from my kitchen filtered through my mind.

As the root violated me, the knife was plunging into her back. I was reliving her pain. Her pain became my pain, as the tree annihilated my opening, branching out into my womb. The blood of *her* mingled with mine, our blood flowed under this spectre of a bleeding tree.

The assault finished abruptly. I felt the jagged branch fidget and wriggle out from within me. The serrated edges took parts of my insides with it, as the root descended back into the garnet sodden earth. I was tattered, blood pooled around my feet. I stood up shakily, my body wracked in pain. I trembled, I twitched and my panties and tights were in shreds. Looking back at the tree that was crimson coated and glowing, I watched it glisten in warm rich blood. Heat emanated from within.

The undulating branches dripped in ruby redness. *It was alive.* The tree had embraced and absorbed itself with the essence of human pain and human emotion. The tree pulsed with the very energy that it took from me. The proud tree had a part of life inside its empty truck. It consumed part of me and part of a murdered woman. In a defiant final quake, the tree shook its final coating of blood, soaking me thoroughly.

I turned my back on the lonely tree. I travelled wearily back to the house, just as I had wearily left the hellish home only hours before. I opened the door to my home once more and faced the carnage that faced me in the kitchen.

With a heavy heart I began to cut my wrists with the bloodied knife that lay bleakly amongst the splattered mess of the woman's remains. I may have felt the elation of gratification for the first time, but the ramification of my dirty deed filled me with such dread. Maybe I was better off dead also.

Hearing my guttural sobs my sister strode into the chaotic room. Flustered and alarmed she dropped the cello case onto the floor, a string plucked as it landed abruptly to the ground. I continued to carve up my wrists.

She gently retrieved the wet knife from my shaking hands cooing with lulling tones as I buried my head into her soft lap that smelt of her 'Anais Anais' perfume. Bless her. She had saved me, but my mundane life was over before it even begun.

***

After years of psychiatric care, I was released. I benefited from the one to one sessions with their caring sympathises. The inquest concluded I was provoked due to mitigating circumstances. Good behaviour pays off in the end. My body now healed from the ruthless assault, I still go back to my tree and give him offerings.

Having now become the owner of the new orphanage built upon the hill overlooking my Lonely Tree, I have the power to provide the tree with its needs and in return it shows me its energising and prevailing love.

The foul tiresome nurse at the institution that irritated me beyond all reasoning now lies beneath these roots, along with the rotting heart. As a childless woman, I now have my own *special* children. I simply take them from their sweet slumber, end their precious life, oh so peacefully may I add and bury them under my tree.

Her inheritance was of some use, though there was a bitter battle regarding if I was sane enough to be in control of it. But I have become so self aware, so confident, so damn selfish. Just like her. She taught me something. She taught me how to get what I want and how to manipulate certain situations and now it has finally come to a head. Or was it my tree that made me who I am today? No matter. It's a blessing for me and a blessing for my tree. My lover gets all he needs from me now.

We are of the same stem.

THE BOYS' NIGHT OUT

Max grinned at himself in the elaborate mirror as he loosened his bowtie. He turned to Greg with an air of arrogance.

"Such a fucking blast! Even some old boys from Harrow joined us, but they can't hack it like us Etonians, we party far better than those dickheads."

Still fuelled with alcohol Max was on a high. He drained the final residue from the champagne bottle.

Greg was leaning over the glass side table, inhaling the thin white lines which lay with military precision side by side. He snorted vulgarly as he inhaled the expensive white powder.

"It was a good bash, not bad for a 'lardy da' do! Shame I didn't get a fucking shag though." Greg retorted with a sneer.

"Tell you what Max," Greg continued, "Shall we go and get *our* sexual thrill and I don't mean shagging. Remember how fantastic it was last time?"

Max stopped preening himself and turned round. A smile emerged from his narrow lips.

"What right now? It's almost midnight!"

"Exactly! More fucking scumbags on the streets mate." Greg scoffed as he retracted the tightly rolled twenty pound note.

Max turned to Kev who sat opposite the Plasma TV staring vacantly at his game.

"You up for it?"

"Sure. These bloody bums need to be taught a lesson. After last time, we can wipe these bleeders off our streets."

Kev got up from the floor, tossed the controls onto the chaise lounge and turned to his friends.

"So. Ready to go guys? After playing Manhunt, I am pumped up for action."

The three men put on their dinner jackets once more and left their prestigious penthouse flat.

***

The snow descended delicately. Dressed in their navy satin lined woollen coats and silver cufflinks, they walked determinedly down London's festive high street. The luminous lights glowed on their features that were now fuelling with a hidden agenda. To the oncoming person, their exterior posed only that of a dignified nature. Polite pillars of society.

***

Finally, huddled against a damp wall under a viaduct, a victim was found. Debris and neglect engulfed the figure. A roaring train whistled overhead drowning any evidence of the approaching men.

"Oi mate! Fancy a ciggie?"

Max focused on the hooded figure, forcing a warm inviting smile.

"I feel for you, mate. Cold this time of year isn't it. Not the best way to spend your evenings is it?"

Whist flicking the lighter repeatedly Max handed out a cigarette. The beggar rose from his dwelling. Unshaven and odorous, his hair covered the majority of his features. His clothes so soiled, it was hard to differentiate between any two colours.

Abruptly, Greg who was lingering behind Max, kicked the man forcefully behind his knees, watching him buckle gleefully. Max swiftly turned around to see if anyone was near. Satisfied, he stamped on the man's knee, cracking the patella with a harsh snap under his Gucci heels. From the shadows, Kev emerged. Max lifted the vagrant from the snowy slush and held him erect.

"Here's my *gift* to you. Happy fucking Christmas, you scum," Max mocked maliciously. "You litter our streets; pollute our lives with your petty worthlessness!"

Spittle sprayed from Max's mouth directly into the vagrant's beard.

Max then grabbed the back of the startled loner's hair that was slippery with grease. Pulling the clammy hair with excessive force, the follicles ripped away from the reddening scalp leaving a large clump of lubricous hair gripped into Max's fist.

"Eat this, you twat!" Max rammed the hair and much of his own fist down the vagrant's throat. The loafer retched. His eyeballs bulged, blood seeping into the milky eyes. Still holding the vagrant upright, Kev began to boot him repeatedly in the ankles.

Observing, Greg began to unbuckle his belt then opened his zip. Caressing his genitals he relished the scene. The thrill *he* was seeking was soon to erupt.

"Hold him steady, Kev!" Max launched his fist into the wanderer's stomach with such force that Kev almost keeled over. Finally he was released, his body thudding into the filth.

The threesome sustained their battering on the loner's body; damaging and beating his form until they began to feel the tinges of exhaustion. The strains of Mistletoe and Wine resonated from a nearby bar. They jeered, thrilling at the audacity of their sport. Elated and orgasmically charged and in spite of their weakening will, they persisted to pound the man's body. Collectively after a moments lull, they urinated upon the convulsing body.

They halted their attack. Zipping up his fly Max shoved Kev aside and raised the wanderer by his shoulders once more, hoisting him up against the dank wall. The other two men exhausted, stood aside.

Grabbing the perishing man's collar, he leaned closer into the shattered, raw face.

With a sudden snort, Max released his grip. The man's body collapsed onto the gory dirt. Max knelt down to the pulverised body and studied him, with a sudden overwhelming acknowledgment consuming him.

The beaten swollen eyes, though damaged, were now recognisable.

One was blue.

One brown.

He smeared the blood away from the pained face and brushed back the sticky hair that coated the blood soaked brow.

"Hugh?"

A groan seeped out from the damaged face.

He looked into the eyes of his brother.

He recalled the day his brother, his best friend left home. After being made redundant from an editorial position, Hugh had simply disappeared. Not a word from him.

Until now.

Max pushed his face closer to his brothers, feeling the hot breath upon his cheek.

"Why Hugh..?"

Hugh sputtered painfully from his mulched mouth.

"I lost everything, you know that. I owed so much. I had to leave. I couldn't face your damning ridicule. You and Dad made me feel so worthless, so…" Hugh began to choke on his own blood and vomit, but continued in spite of the state of his traumatised body and mind.

"But now I see what you represent. You judgmental arrogant bastard! God, I am *glad* I am not like you *ANYMORE!*"

Hugh weakly but precisely, plunged the hidden blade deep into his brother's femoral artery; thick arterial blood spurted from the wound, viscous dark fluid poured over the scarlet stained slush. Hugh's life eventually ebbed away.

Max died gazing into the eyes of his brother. Together, they died entwined, in death's lasting embrace.

SHALLOW CRIES

Cold winter rain sharply lashed at the window. The wind lulled temporarily.

Sam's laughter reverberated through the room as he pushed the remote control rigidly in the hope his car would gain more speed.

The room was a blush of soft light. Flames flickered and danced from the hearth, smoke and fire marrying in unison. A perfect chorus of snaps and crackling firewood filled the air, the pungent earthy scent of wood and charcoal hung in the atmosphere, circulating liberally.

The logs splintered and hissed as Tony sat with his back to the warmth and security of the radiant heat. With a hint of competitiveness, he enthusiastically challenged his son. The cars buzzed and whizzed around the track frantically.

Framed smiling faces that adorned the mantelpiece glowed with beguiling vivacity. The steady tick from the antique Westminster mantle clock was starkly interrupted by sombre but lyrical chords that subtly dispersed throughout the room.

"Bath time, Sam." Tony uttered to his son as he drained the remaining residue of his Vodka and Lemonade. He noticed his distorted features through the arc of colour that was held within the crystal glass. He flicked a stray lock of hair that had carelessly fallen across his lined but handsome face.

His dark chestnut hair now contained fragments of grey that enhanced and framed his angular face.

"Aw...no Dad!" Sam moaned challengingly. He lowered his head in a sulk, but obediently reached out for the box and began packing the tracks and cars away. His hair curled around his green eyes, his honey highlights shimmering in the luminosity of the room.

Sam was a smart nine year old. At an age of self awareness he often was temperamental and capricious but Tony enjoyed their intimate times together. Nothing could come between them. Sam was Tony's life.

***

Mari sat silently by a table where a glass bowl of potpourri emanated a gentle bouquet.

She remained still as she felt an unyielding love for the child she was watching. She savoured the vision that was before her, an overwhelming desire and longing folded from within, united with the true horror of the knowledge that she would never hold Sam again.

Though she was no longer a physical being, she accepted this ethereal existent. She was able to watch her son in all avenues of his life.

The craving and regret of the absence of physical contact plagued Mari to a degree of obsession. She'd often gaze at her sleeping son and would hum a melody for him if he awoke suddenly, which he often did, overcoming the final threads of a nightmare. She longed to bury her nose in his neck and nestle into him, to feel his breath upon her face.

She missed his spontaneous need for her. However, she cherished what she saw, she could see him and that was a blessing, however small. Sam was too old to yearn for her now, she was a mere distant thought of a time gone by, but she still implored his love; the pain inside her besieging her constantly.

***

Sam finally placed the lid on the tatty box. He got to his feet and went into the alcove of the kitchen which was adjacent to the living room, and then joined his father who was pouring himself yet another drink.

"You coming up, Dad?" enquired Sam.

"You stay here and load these plates into the dishwasher and I will run your bath, OK?"

Tony took a decadent gulp of his drink, refilled his glass then turned to leave the kitchen.

"Ok Dad, see you up there."

Tony ran up the stairs, two at a time. The spacious Victorian rooms were not consistent with the narrow stairway and halls. His pace reduced as he got to the top of the stairs. He faced the looming hall, where the bathroom awaited him. He hated this hall, its slim corridor ominous in the dim artificial light. But it wasn't the oppressive gloom that left him so unsettled.

As he purposefully strode down the corridor a sudden excruciating memory resurfaced. The pinnacle of the haunting recollection intensified as he entered the bathroom.

Tony searched for the plastic crocodile that twisted around the light cord. It bounced onto his elbow as he blindly swiped the air.

The string had been lengthened for Sam in the hope that he would eventually venture into the bathroom alone at night, but he still, to this day found it an insufferable experience. At bath times he insisted that his father sat on the large wicker chair at the back of the blue tiled bathroom, so he would not feel isolated. Tony did this dutifully but with reluctance.

He finally pulled the cord; stark vivid light sparked a raw remembrance of the night that altered his life forever, leaving this room as a dark iconic cloud that would fester in his mind, always.

***

Mari watched as Sam attentively loaded the dishwasher. She beseeched her son to be able to see her, acknowledge her. She was desperate to hold him and inhale the aroma of his scalp but her arms held no substance. Her feelings were so intense that it almost made her feel complete; complete with heart; with breath; with totality.

Circling around Sam she grabbed desperately but fruitlessly to touch his skin, his soft downy hair, his body.

***

A faint eddy of wind alerted Sam. He looked around to see if a window was ajar; all were closed. He finished loading the final plate, double checked the room in case he had left an item unaccounted for. Feeling chilled, he swiftly finished his job by getting the cleaning tablet and placed it into the machine. It rumbled into life as Sam turned it on.

***

Mari's feeling of powerless solitude consumed her. She took a step back reluctantly, her arms dropped limply by her side. The dark memory came to the forefront of her mind. A recollection so disquieting she chose to banish it immediately. She turned from her son grudgingly as she turned into the hall. Ascending the stairs she heard the familiar sounds that were coming from the bathroom, her feelings dipping into a pit of heavy-heartedness.

***

"Dad, done it, I'm coming, just getting something!"

Sam yelled loudly up to his father as he bounded up the stairs. But his voice was now drowned by the running water, which gushed loudly and splurged from the ageing taps.

Tony knelt down as he poured the bubble bath into the running water. In spite of the warm vapour that was forming around him, he felt bitterly cold. He rubbed the back of his neck to try and eradicate the sudden chill.

Glancing over to the mirror he noticed that it was starting to fog with condensation. A dark smudgy faceless form gazed back at him; he felt an unnerving aura surrounding him. This familiar yet terrifying presence once again lingered with Tony as he pushed himself up. He exited the bathroom at speed.

Behind the door Mari watched him depart. She began to lift her arms to grab him, but dropped them suddenly and lowered her head.

She took a pace out of the door and her eyes followed Tony as he met Sam coming along the murky hall.

***

"Going to get ready now, dad. I will get my water pistol and we can have a fight!" Sam enthusiastically ran to his bedroom. Agreeing, Tony wandered into his bedroom.

Here he turned on his bedside radio; the muted sounds of conversation had a welcoming affect on him. He sat on the king-size bed as he often did and looked at the empty space that lay vacant next to him. The vodka now taking a negative effect intensified his senses and also his brooding memories.

***

Mari hovered in the hallway and watched Sam as he retrieved his pistol and left his room. He hesitated and loitered in the doorway of the bathroom. He turned back to call for his father.

***

"Dad, come on!" Sam was insistent as he stood waiting for his father on the landing. Tony eventually emerged from his room.

"Come on, get in there will you!" Tony's voice held some slight irritation as he marched Sam into the middle of the bathroom.

"I can't babysit you every time you have a bath, Sam. You are getting too old for this." Tony slumped into the large chair, feeling his body sink into the embracing wicker fibres.

Sam now naked, turned off both taps and placed his foot cautiously into the water.

"Ok, Dad. When I'm ten, I should be fine then shouldn't I?"

Tony smirked and sipped his drink silently, the alcohol now warming him, but not eradicating his anxiety totally.

The phone rang; its shrill cry broke the sound of the rippling undulating water that came from around Sam's body as he lowered himself into the bath.

"Well you can start by practising now, as I answer that bloody phone." Levering himself out of the chair Tony moved clumsily to the door.

Sam protested noisily, splashing with frustration and annoyance as his father departed.

***

Mari stood opposite the bath, watching Sam as he began to panic due to his father's absence.

It was this moment as she watched Sam in his vulnerable isolation; she re-lived the fateful day, six years ago.

***

When Mari had delivered her twin sons prematurely after thirty weeks gestation; Jamie's lungs were under developed, causing major problems at the start of his precious life. He soldiered on, defying the doubts of the doctors. Sam's heart had been littered with holes. He endured open heart surgery when he was twelve months old. But being a strong wilful individual, he survived the gruelling ordeal. The stress and incomprehensible agony traumatised both parents. They lived, breathed, existed, only in the knowledge that the children had to survive. The boys had battled all of their afflictions with great strength, though there were times when things were very strained. Mari and Tony were so vigilant about the state of their children's health and wellbeing; it caused friction and often opened a rift between them.

When the twins had reached the age of three, things began to settle down. The compulsion to watch every move lessened, but only slightly.

The twin boys had been happily bathing. Jamie caught Sam innocently on the eye with his toy boat. The sharp plastic pierced Sam's delicate pale skin, blood surfacing from the laceration. Blood dribbled down Sam's body, gracing his pale skin with cherry streaks. Swiftly Mari had wrapped him up in a towel and carried him to her bedroom to find the first aid box.

Alone, Jamie began to cough; gently at first and then he began to gasp desperately. An excruciating pain formed within his chest, crushing him as he tried to breathe. The asthma attack left him choking, thrashing and gulping for air. His cries were useless, as the gushing tap drowned out his pitiful pleas. When Mari returned, his small lifeless body floated face down, thudding softly and rhythmically against the side of the bath, the water still holding the evidence of his desperate struggles.

Days later, Mari lay in her own tepid bath water. The same bath that cradled her son's final moments. She closed her eyes as her mind swam with the constant guilt that consumed her. Appearing suddenly, her husband stormed into the bathroom. He hovered above her with an expression of hostility. His eyes held no clue of what was to come. She attempted to sit up.

Grabbing her hair with sudden aggression, he abruptly smashed her head repeatedly against the unforgiving porcelain surface, her skull yielding with every impact. Intense agony *shot through every nerve, blood circled and swirled within the perfumed soap suds and bath water, her struggles were useless.*

"Murderer!" he shrieked maniacally. His wretched face a mask of rage as he held her head beneath the fragrant water. Her last memory of her husband was the utter hatred behind his frenzied eyes, a glare of insanity that penetrated her being as he continued to demolish her head.

Her life ebbed away like dispersing steam; no heavenly light welcomed her; only a single disturbing, guilty truth. It was her cataclysmic error that cost her, her life and that of her son, Jamie.

Tony was found guilty for the horrendous crime he had committed and received three years for manslaughter with mitigating circumstances taken into consideration. He had freely and openly admitted his guilt.

Sam's grandmother had nurtured him in those testing years, here in this very house.

Tony had written daily to his son as he sat within confining walls.

He patiently had waited for the time he would be part of his son's life once more. Eventually, as a free man, he returned to the family home that harboured his ugly deed.

Here Mari was caught in the perpetual state of purgatory. Protectively, she watched over her son. It was the least she could do but the most she could hope for. Mari's choice was to remain here for her growing child. Her guilt so paramount, she was content to exist in this suspended oblivion.

Sam now sat alone. A dripping tap was his only companion. He strained to hear his fathers muffled voice from downstairs. The phone call was lasting for far too long…

Mari gazed at Sam intently, imploringly; hating to see her only surviving son alone in the water.

Mari walked to the side of the bath; the compulsive wish for her son to be safe and secure consumed her. She desperately but silently insisted to Sam that he would be fine. Daddy would be back to play a water fight, once he was off the phone…

***

Sam was about to call for his father when a sudden grey pallor shadowed his face. The vision of his putrefying decaying mother staggering towards him, terrified him. Her eyes were absent of life, they were hollow vacant abysses of blackness. This was too much for the child.

His heart failing with shock he desperately reached out his slender arm. Helplessly seeking assistance, he had no strong arms to reach down to pull him away from his impending death. No supple bosom of security awaited him, to protect him from the undeniable doom. Only an unknown terrifying horror.

Sam's agonised screams called out his brother's name but his squeals became imperceptible as he uttered his last strangled plea. His once zestful but nimble being, now devoid of life sank to the bottom of the deep foamy bath like a heavy leaden weight. His hair haloed around him as the water cupped his fragile corpse.

***

Beholding the vision before her, and yet another death for which she felt wholly responsible, Mari descended into her final torturous hell. Her son ascended into an eternal peace that she so yearned for.

Trapped in the most personal of hells, she could only reflect on this pivotal moment for eternity, knowing that everything she had loved so deeply so desperately, was lost forever.

Her silent screams echoed and absorbed within the fabric of the building, leaving a penetrating pulse of horror and grief that marooned itself within the foundations of this once, happy family home.

IT'S A DOG'S LIFE

"Mum, Please I don't want to go out. It's still raining and..." Nick took a deep breath, wiped his nose and continued in a whining tone. "...and Mum, what if *he's* still out there!"

"Don't be such a drip, Nick. We are totally out of bread and milk and I have loads of washing to finish, so go on honey, please!" Tina shook off the droplets of water from her damp hands as she placed the final potato into the pan.

"Eddy Evans' mum won't let him out to play in the yard just in case he comes back!"

Nick fiddled with some dirt that was embedded into his bitten fingernail, waiting for his mothers reply.

"Look Nick, He's gone now. I am sure of it, sweetie. It was probably a junkie high on dope. Anyone who finds joy attacking lonely men and animals must be on something lethal I'd say." Tina concluded, ruffling her son's hair with her now dry hands and smiled reassuringly. She then continued,

"The last attack was months ago; you will be fine. It's only a ten minute walk; call me on your mobile if you see anything suspicious. You need milk on your Cheerio's anyway and with the change you can get something for yourself, OK?"

With that, Nick surfaced a wry smile as he grabbed the money from the work unit and walked towards the back door.

"But be careful, Nick and keep your eyes open just in case."

"OK Mum, I will. You can be sure of that!"

The traffic blared past Nick as he lumbered down the road, groaning with irritation.

I shouldn't be here if there is a mad man about! However the thought of some toffee popcorn banished his fears temporarily as his stomach growled like a young kitten in need for its mummy's warm milk.

Rain continued to splatter Nick as he wandered past the old abandoned warehouse. Shadowy windows loomed down on him, some intact, some smashed revealing their nasty jagged teeth. Nick shuddered as he noticed a fleeting movement swift past one of the open entrances. His stomach flipped when he suddenly heard a pitiful yowl coming from behind a turned over dustbin that was adjacent to one of the darkened doorways. His curiosity stung him like tips of icy crystals forming deep within his head, his fingertips twitched with unease.

His love for animals was paramount. In his eleven years of life he had already mapped out his future. His aim was to achieve the adequate qualifications and become a vet.

Reluctantly though dutifully, and in spite of the pull of fear that developed inside him, he walked towards the pathetic wail. He wandered towards the stern gateway that led to the grounds of the warehouse.

The ground crunched crisply under his footfalls. Aiming for the rusty dustbin, Nick glimpsed a tiny paw shaking from behind the corroded steel.

Beyond lay the main entrance that led into the deserted building, its hungry mouth gaping open ready for its next meal. Nick shuddered at the thought, cross with himself for being so scared. His imagination always got the better of him. As Nick approached the whimpering animal the creature flinched, edging away from his outstretched hands. The puppy shook as Nick smoothly knelt down to comfort the distressed animal.

"Shhh, come on, boy. I ain't gonna hurt you buddy, honest."

As Nick spoke, the little pup dashed along the gravelled path and straight into the open mouth of the dark entrance.

"Freakin' hell!" Nick muttered under his breath. Annoyed that he had spoken too loudly and frightened the little stray pup away; he tentatively followed the animal as it became absorbed into the darkness of the desolate building. Nick looked behind him to make sure he wasn't being followed and walked into the echoic murky building; he shuddered as he entered the darkness.

"Come on boy, where are you?" His voice was small within the large empty building. Nick was now feeling jumpy as his footsteps were the only sound that resonated around him. No sign of the pup.

No wailing or whimpering greeted Nick this time. The silence was killing him, accentuating his loneliness within the foreboding building.

A sound suddenly came from underneath the large staircase that stood imposingly in the middle of the vast derelict lobby, alerting Nick that he was now not alone. Fragments of sunlight flooded through the vast shattered window that was erected above the top of the decaying stairway. This gave Nick enough light to see the tiny puppy dart from the darkness and into the middle of the hallway. Running past Nick, the dog then stopped in its tracks. The erectile hair on the puppy's back stood firm, then it immediately scampered to crouch behind the remains of a reception desk as Nick quietly approached.

Deciding not to say anything, Nick simply sat on the dusty soiled floor and stretched his arms out in an open gesture of reassurance.

The puppy finally shuffled its tiny paws towards Nick, its ears drawn back with its tail limply hanging between its legs.

"See, I'm not all bad. It's OK, buddy. I ain't gonna hurt you."

The pup nuzzled his cold nose against Nick's neck, its little heart rampantly beating as the friends began to bond.

***

Malevolent eyes watched the boy and his new companion as they clutched each other in the throes of a new found friendship. A feeling of annoyance rushed through the quivering body, as the stranger walked away from the window. After watching the loving scene from the outside cracked and murky window, enticing feelings of wrath and anger surfaced. It was time to do some more hunting, cleanse the world from vermin.

***

"…Yes, it was about a month ago. The community is still on alert, but don't worry Maggie. Things have quietened down now. No need to worry anymore." Terry Marks retold his sister the events regarding the brutal attacks on solitary men and stay feral dogs.

"…and they say it's a rabid dog that's doing all this, or some sick bastard. No evidence leads to the fact it's a man, but between you and me, I am convinced it is, sis. Must be some kind of sicko, Maggie. The way they are ripped apart…" Terry finished his conversation wearily, feeling a wave of depression wash over him. After his goodbyes Terry replaced the phone back onto its cradle.

The heat was getting to him, especially as he had just cycled the five mile journey from his accounts office. At sixty one years of age, Terry was not in the best of health, high blood pressure being the fundamental concern. Living alone wasn't easy either, he wished his dearest Mary was still with him. She would always coo to him in order to calm his nerves, as she handed him a nip of whiskey. She had done this religiously each evening when he came in from work.

God, how he missed his beautiful wife.

Sighing heavily, he reached for his address book to call his doctor. It was time to increase his medication; a check up would be a good idea. Settling down into the pine chair that was placed next to the phone table, he flicked through the book using his finger. As he did so, a movement caught his eye from outside his living room window. A flash of beige material flickered past as he narrowed his eyes to focus more clearly. Nothing. Terry shrugged his shoulders and continued to search for the number.

After a few moments he suddenly heard the jangle of keys as his back door opened. Someone was walking into his sterile kitchen. His head pounding, Terry felt his blood pressure surge through his veins as he stood up to investigate. He hesitated in the doorway. Walking out into the hallway he fell to his knees as the hatchet embedded into his pink smooth hairless head, blood pooling around him as his last thoughts fell into an abyss of pain.

"*Mary, help me…*"

***

Nick cupped the puppy into his arms as he searched for a substitute lead. He couldn't walk into the shop holding a dog, so in an effort to find a perfect implement, Nick wandered out into the fresh air inhaling the purer atmosphere. The rain had left a heavy scent of dampness in the air. Shimmering sun cut into the grey clouds causing pockets of coloured light falling into the rainbow puddles that were scattered randomly around him.

Searching through the overgrown grounds that were littered with abandoned chairs and old empty crates that were spilling over with weeds; he eventually found some old thin shoddy rope. Creating a loose loop he carefully placed it around the puppy's neck, making sure it was not too tight. The last thing he wanted to do was choke the little thing. Taking one final look around him, he left the forsaken warehouse and its grounds and walked back onto the pavement and headed towards the small store on the corner.

***

"A pint of milk is it? Here you go, honey. Anything else?" The cheery attendant smiled sweetly. Her robust face flushed with life, ready and willing to serve the polite boy beyond her counter.

"Some popcorn, please." Ethel reached under the counter and handed over her best selling corn that she prepared herself on the premises.

"Here you go, honey, and ain't *he* a cutie!" She ushered with her eyes into the direction where the small brown puppy sat obediently outside. Nick had secured the rope on the railing that was a perfect place to leave his little friend.

"Got a name, has he?"

"No, I only just found him, he's a stray. I am gonna take him home, give him something to eat and see if mum will let me keep him." Nick followed Ethel as she walked from behind her counter and headed for the adorable animal.

The puppy retreated at first, but as soon as Ethel's warm big hands stroked the matting fur, the pup rolled on its back and devoured the attention it so sorely missed.

"Where you find him?" Ethel asked inquisitively.

"At the old warehouse, the empty one opposite." Nick answered as she continued to swamp the dog with affection.

As she heard Nick's words, she suddenly stopped.

"You didn't go in *there* did you, alone?"

"Yes, I did. The animal was crying, shaking. I had to find out if I could help him and well…he's here now so what's the problem?" Nick's voice was tainted with irritability and unease. He hated being questioned.

"Just listen to my words, kiddo; you don't go there again, OK? Some strange things have been found in there, things kids like you should never see."

To add emphasis to her chilling words, a police siren boomed past the two of them as they looked on, watching it swerve past the moving traffic.

For a dog so young, the puppy walked well on its makeshift lead. Splashing in the shallow puddles, Nick was glad to be heading for home.

"What an adventure we have had, dude. Don't cha think? I mean, what with these strange animal killings and such, it's lucky I found you when I did. You're a lucky fella, you know that?"

Nick held the lead tightly in one hand as he held the plastic bag of bread, milk and popcorn in the other. Nick was eager to get indoors and to munch on his popcorn with his new pal by his side.

"I have a name for you. I think I will call you *'Lucky'*, seeing as you *so* are!"

Nick laughed out loud at his witty remark as he turned the final corner that led to his house.

Approaching the driveway Nick felt a creeping grip of anxiety. What if his mum wouldn't allow him to have this new pet?

He turned down to the side of his house that lead to the back door. The door was open. The small net curtain flapped in the light wind as did the door, causing it to bang against the wooden frame.

Silence greeted the pair.

"Mum, I have a surprise. Mum?"

Nick walked into the deserted kitchen. There was no sign of Tina, no sound to indicate that she was near.

His visits to his mum's were seldom, but indeed very special. Living with his father for the majority of the year had proved testing for him. He had missed her desperately. The divorce however, was inevitable. Life together with both parents also had been a trying time. Reasons unbeknown to him, this was the best option.

"Mum. You there?" Nick quizzed impatiently,

"I've got the milk. Mum!"

As he reached the kitchen table his heart jolted. Lying in a puddle of scarlet congealing blood was a hatchet. Beads of ruby fluid dripped off the table like droplets from a gemmed necklace. A thin trail of blood continued to descend down the table leading towards the hall. Nick grabbed Lucky in complete disbelief, his insides turning into rippling liquid. The track of blood stopped at a closed door.

The bathroom door.

With a shaking hand and a throat full of sickly acid, Nick opened the door slowly.

"Mum, you OK?" Fear fingered its chilling clinch around Nick, as he thought about the man people were talking about.

He's here?

Nick was not prepared for the vision that awaited him. The bathroom was awash with dripping blood. The shower curtain was splattered with traces of fur and crimson syrup. Fragments of tissue lay on the floor callously thrown into a heaped gooey mess. With matted blood soaked fur, a creature was being skinned; its fresh frayed flesh was being guzzled by a kneeling figure. The figure masticated with ferocity as it supped and sucked on the animal's carcass. As the form turned around, Nick dropped Lucky in complete panic as his mother sneered back at him with a blood coated grimace.

"Sorry Nick you had to find out this way. *They* tell me it's my duty; I will be the one that is saved, Nick. I am cleansing society sweetheart, it has to be done."

The water rushed from the shower hissing and steaming as the cerise water spiralled down the plug hole. She continued in a more heated tone. "The mass of males polluting our town *have* to be removed."

"Men and dogs. Both the same in my eyes, Nick. They are out there to hump everything, even that scabby dog of yours. I don't want you to turn out like that Nick; I have to protect you, matey. *They* tell me it's a necessity. I didn't want you to find out, but now that you do, you and that soppy eyed mongrel better come here…"

   Nick's mother stood up and stepped out of the shower in her blood coated nudity. She followed her fleeing son through into the kitchen; picking up the hatchet as she ran through the house.

THE CHRISTMAS CURSE

Jessie embraced her new sobriety. Having spent three months in rehab for abusing drugs, the blood that pulsed within her body was pure and cleansed. She could actually feel the rush of hope gush through her veins as she swelled with hopefulness.

Today she would not be lonely. Today she would see a friend, and the isolation would be a thing of the past.

Solitude was her only grievance since recovering from the claws of addiction that had consumed her since she was nineteen.

She had lost all respect from her family and her close friends. Even though she was a different and stronger woman, she was still stigmatised by those who she thought she could trust. Those that encouraged her to walk the road of destruction only saw her infrequently, but now, with a new promising life ahead of her, she steered clear from those that led her into that chasm of obliteration.

The radio alarm clock abruptly interrupted her thoughts with the sound of angelic voices filling the bedroom with Christmas cheer, reflecting her mellow and contented mood. It was four days until Christmas and today she was going to meet her new friend Ian for the first time. They had first met online, sending each other words of encouragement, as Ian was also a recovering addict.

How she hated that label.

Jessie had soon begun to feel the fluttering thrill whenever she thought of Ian. She was starting to fall in love, and the feeling was mutual much to Jessie's joy.

Stretching her legs, she slid out of her warm nest of slumber. She walked to the window and opened the curtains, the joyous carols still ringing through her room as she looked out. Snow started to fall randomly like delicate jewels of crystal upon her window pane. Things really did look magical; she felt it surround her. Today, things would be different.

Jumping onto the bus, she brushed off the loose snowflakes from her coat as she sat down. The journey was not long. Finally reaching her destination, a feeling of nervousness fleeted through her, a mild sense of trepidation lingered a little too long for her liking as she walked through the library doors.

They had planned to meet at the paranormal section of the library. Ian had a keen interest in all things anomalous and luckily so did Jessie. She searched for Ian fruitlessly. After fifteen minutes Jessie took out her mobile. A deep plummeting feeling of disappointment started to encircle her as she punched the digits with her shaking fingers. Only a dead line greeted her.

Jessie now frustrated, got up and turned to leave, but as she did so, a thin lady with a large decorative turban blocked her path. In an abrupt manner she said, "He can't make it, but he left you this."

Thrusting the object into her hands, Jessie examined the item. Looking up to confront the stranger, Jessie could see she already had disappeared.

Staggered Jessie sat down at a table; she opened up the brown oblong box. She raised the small metal catch, and lifted the pine lid. It was an Ouija board. Slamming the lid down harshly, Jessie strode out of the library and with hot tears pinching at her eyes; she jumped back onto the number 84 bus.

Jessie felt deflated as she sat at the back of the bus. She watched a courting couple cuddle up to each other, the young boy stroking his lover's blonde hair, then kissed the tip of her nose. A feeling of sorrowfulness filled her heavy heart like a flooding room. A yearning for companionship grabbed her.

***

Sitting down with a strong coffee, she opened the Ouija board that sat in front of her. The board was stunningly beautiful. Gold and ebony supernatural images adorned the surface. A planchette in the middle sat upon black letters and numbers.

Not knowing what to do, but going on what she had seen on TV, she placed her finger lightly on the planchette and asked a question in a hushed tone.

"Hello, anyone there?" Her voice broke the deathly silence.

Slowly the dial moved. Amazed Jessie felt the dial glide over the letters. The subtle scratching of the indicator was the only sound detectable. The words spelt out;

"Ian is here with me."

"Where is *here?*" Jessie asked perplexed.

"Inside me. Join him."

Shocked Jessie nearly spilt the coffee as she removed her finger abruptly from the wooden dial. Waves of fear channelled within her.

Unexpectedly the dial moved by itself erratically. Whispering echoes of many voices hovered at the edge of perception. Jessie gasped. Her chair suddenly lifted from the floor throwing her to the ground. The TV blasted on as every light in her flat starkly radiated from the bulbs.

The sofa glided across the room, knocking over the small Christmas tree, scattering the room in baubles and tinsel. The kitchen and bathroom taps roared into life as the carols blared from the radio.

Almost every object shuddered or fell to the ground.

Jessie screamed, and yelled, "*WHO ARE YOU? WHY ARE YOU DOING THIS? WHERE IS IAN?*"

All objects suddenly stilled as an emerging eddy of grey mist ascended from the board, chilling the room. It rose so high, it hovered only inches from the ceiling. A sibilant but beguiling voice surfaced from within the milky fog.

"*He is here with us, come join him in this blissful curse, Jessie. Join us and you never will feel the ache of self doubt and loneliness again, give in to your temptations and you can be free. Surrender your weakness for lasting peace of mind.*"

"But I am at *peace* now, I don't NEED this!" Jessie shrieked.

Grabbing the box in frantic haste, Jessie ran from her ransacked bed-sit, away from the blatant enticement. How simple it would be to join Ian and to seal the cavity within her, but she *had* beaten all alluring temptations. She would never go back there again.

Jessie ran into the snowy street. Turning her head behind her in the desperate hope that the entity was nowhere in sight, she ran blindly into a group of boisterous youths.

As the thief ran into her, his blade sunk into her heart. With one plunge the sharpened metal fell into the soft fabric of Jessie's flesh, death greeted her swiftly. She fell to the ground, her blood staining the purity of the soft snow, leaving a red aura around her head.

A passing child on his bicycle witnessed the tragic event. The huddle of thieves dispersed rapidly like fleeing sheep.

Reluctant to attend to the dying girl, the youngster grabbed the box that lay abandoned upon the milky pavement.

A lady with a turban watched on quietly from the other side of the road. She started to smile as the young teen opened the box.

THE HAND THAT FEEDS

Washing the final traces of residue that stained her supple body, Simone turned off the shower. She stepped outside and reached for the plush warm towel that awaited her on the heated rail. Wrapping the luxurious fabric around herself, she inhaled the delicate fragrance of flower-blossom. Memories of her painful childhood nudged her back into reality. Her mother often used this brand of fabric conditioner. Opening her eyes she stared at herself in the bathroom mirror. *Like Father, like daughter,* she smirked to herself as she recalled her night of passion with the client that still lay warm in the bed next door.

Reaching for the other smaller towel Simone tilted her head forward and wrapped it around her head into a turban. Cooing a gentle song she dried herself off completely.

"…Cause something happened to me while I was driving home and I'm not the same anymore…"

Burt Bacharach always made Simone feel so much better.

***

Entering the bedroom that was decorated in elaborate Edwardian wallpaper, Simone swiftly slipped on her panties, bra and cream tailored suit.

Looking back at the bed, the rumpled sheets concealed Mr. Tom Blake. His large round frame, mountainous under the black silken sheets, lay motionless. Simone continued to prepare for her exit, finally applying ruby red lipstick onto her full mouth. Scraping her auburn hair back in a tight French bun, Simone finally went over to the bed.

"Tommy, I am going now, don't forget about our little friend. He still may well be in the covers. Sorry about the mess, but I have sincerely had the most passionate of times. Call me."

Simone laughed with menacing malice as she picked up her handbag and a small canvas holdall. Walking towards the door, Simone scanned the room once more as the tiny rodent ran from under the blood soaked valance.

***

"Yes of course. Mr...?" Simone enquired as she clutched the phone; "...Ok, you don't have to give me your real name. I will meet you at the Vine Hotel at eight o' clock. Yes, Brandi is my name."

Putting the phone back into the cradle, Simone then walked towards her cellar door. Drawing back the bolt, steep dark steps descended into the bowels of the basement. In spite of the darkness Simone knew every step. She made this journey regularly. Reaching the final step she found the light switch. Amber light flooded the dusty neglected hovel.

The chest freezer stood against the bare gas pipes that were shrouded in cobwebs. Next to the huge freezer a cage contained a mischief of albino rats which wriggled and clustered within their restricting space. Their high pitched squeak was barely audible within the silent room. The only noise evident was the hum of the freezer. An empty rocking chair sat vacant at the back of the dingy room. Its large wooden back and edges were decoratively carved with vine leafs and grapes. There were no layers of dust evident on this mahogany chair. A cushion and a blanket lay on the side, adorned in a tapestry of scarlet and green swirls.

Inhaling the putrid odour Simone gagged on the stale air. Nevertheless she breathed a sigh of relief knowing that she was alone. Walking towards the freezer, she opened the colossal lid with one arm. Here she was greeted with trophies. Blood splattered freezer bags of severed hands lay heaped together haphazardly. Picking up the bag with 'Blake' labelled in italic and immaculate writing, Simone recalled her night of passion with Tommy. He *was* tender. So very gentle in spite of his hulky weight and the excessive sweat that leaked from every pore as he heaved inside her. Simone felt loved for a split second.

For an *iota* of a second.

She recalled her painful days as a child. Memories riddled within her like a cancer. By having these hands in her possession she finally felt a glimmer of accomplishment, she has indeed been a good girl.

***

"A gin and tonic please." John ordered Simone's favourite beverage. She would always have this tipple when she was working.

"I am always discreet don't worry, John. I will leave at dawn and no one will have known I ever existed. Just pay me up front and I will show you the time of your life then 'whoosh' I am gone like a bird in flight."

Simone captivated John Baxter, his manhood throbbed with anticipation. Her creamy complexion was a blush with a cherry glow, accentuating her emerald green eyes, filling him with a desire he had never experienced before in his opulent life.

"Good. The last thing I want is for my company to find out about you. I want you all to myself, lock you away and ravish you all day long!" John laughed awkwardly as Simone's smile faded into an expressionless slash.

"You OK? Sorry I didn't mean to offend you..." John continued, "I was only joking Brandi!"

Simone cleared her throat and forced her professional smile back onto her perfectly chiselled face.

"John, no worries, sorry. After our drinks, let's go to the room. You retire first and I will follow fifteen minutes later. Don't want others seeing us leaving together now do we!" She chuckled as she caressed her opened toed sandal against John's ankle.

"Oooh, you are a little minx. I can't wait to get down to business!" John smirked as he drowned the remainder of his single malt whiskey.

***

Their bodies clammy after a session of bland sex, Simone sat up and lit a cigarette. Half-heartedly she uttered under the coils of smoke.

"So you managed it didn't you. You are still a man. You can now go back to your wife proud. Your little soldier stood well to attention. See you had a hang up, that's all. You are not impotent and no need for Viagra."

"Well I guess you do it for me, girl. My wife doesn't obviously. I am going to have to ask for you again you know that don't you?" John panted as he wriggled his wrists that were constrained within handcuffs that he had brought willingly himself.

Leaning over to reach the bedside table, she pulled out a hacksaw from within the draw. Without a word Simone straddled John, gripping his sides hard with her powerful thighs. John's sentence was never finished as she began to saw at his wrists violently and mechanically. Her naked body now a canvas of claret, she finally carved into the final threads of tissue. The hand limply fell onto the bed, bouncing off John's ample stomach. John's eyes were wide, shock disabling him from speaking or even screaming.

From under the bed Simone reached for a bag that she had placed there only hours before. From within the muslin bag, a tin box lay neatly at the bottom. A freezer bag sat snugly against it, along side the black marker pen and sticky label. Delving into the box that had ten holes pierced into it, Simone pulled out the fancy rat. It's twitching nose desperately inhaling the fresh air and the fresh scent of blood.

Letting the rat free, it scuttled under the blood-soaked bed clothes. Simone let the rat do what a rat does best.

Waste not want not.

John finally did scream, but as soon as his scream left his throat, Simone held the pillow firmly against his face. His head and body erupted with spasms of chaotic twitches as his life finally ended in an explosion of pain and suffering.

Her job done, Simone hoisted herself off the now limp corpse and lifted the hand from the bed. Placing it into the freezer bag gently, she sealed the bag closed. She used the black marker pen and named and dated the sticky label, sticking it carefully onto the freezer bag. Placing all articles back into the muslin sling bag once more, Simone went into the en suite and enjoyed her hot steamy shower. The rat continued to squirm under the bedclothes feasting on the most tender parts of John's dead body.

***

After her shower she dressed and put on her makeup. Before she left, she sat quietly and pensively for a long time. The full moon silhouetted her form from within the darkened room. Here Simone began to brood. She thought about her latest trick, and how she needed a change. It was getting too tricky. In her leather handbag the rolls of £50 notes graced her purse once more, but it was blood money for sure, though she did get to wear the best clothes and go to the best restaurants.

Sighing, Simone got up and then she remembered the handcuffs, her finger prints were smeared all over them. Going back to the bathroom, she got a towel and wiped all artefacts that she had touched within the room. Simone waited another hour and left the hotel, when all was at its quietest.

***

Entering her home in the early hours, all was still. Her house consumed in darkness now incurred some haunting memories, the same continued haunting memories that had never left her...

If only her mother was still alive.

Exhausted she turned on the kitchen light. Her first glance was to the cellar door. She knew what she had to do; she had to make the journey down to the cellar and into the dour grimy room where the freezer awaited. But first she needed a strong drink.

She reached for her bag and pulled out the single hand. Clutching it to her breast she made her way down the dark staircase. As she neared the final step, she heard a cackle. She knew that *he* had returned. She could feel his stare even through the dark ebony inkiness of the room. She reached for the switch. To confirm her growing fear, he sat there in the carved mahogany rocking chair, the rhythmic creak of his moving weight puncturing the fragile silence. He sat motionless now, only his lips twitching. Eager to be told of his offering from his daughter, he smacked his lips together.

"So my girl, did you do well tonight? What have you got me? Even in my blindness I can smell your money and the blood you try to conceal. But that's not a worry. I hope the money is safe Simone. So, any offerings today? Anyone give you their hand in marriage?"

The man guffawed raucously as he laughed at his own pathetic joke. The light that hung limply from the shabby electrical wire reflected within his black dusty sunglasses. His bald head glistened with sweat as he continued to laugh.

Simone eventually managed to speak.

"Yes, Daddy, I have a hand for you. I know how you love them grilled, but tonight I am too fucking tired to cook, so if you will excuse me, I must sleep. Earning you this money, fulfilling your dirty deeds and keeping you safe away from the police is taking it out on me."

"YOU DO AS YOU ARE TOLD OR I WILL BLIND YOU AS YOU BLINDED ME!"

Her father roared with such ferocity that Simone physically shook, just as she did as a child.

***

Simone reluctantly recalled the moment she jarred the screwdriver into his eyes as he molested her when she was seventeen years old. It was a terrifying moment, but she knew he was a murderous monster and he was now violating her. The tool shed had proved to be his favourite haunt. As a rat catcher by profession, he spent many an hour dealing out poisons and making traps. No-one suspected his evil doings, only Simone knew what he was up to.

But enough was enough, Simone rammed the screwdriver so hard into his eyes that the jellied membranes burst and splattered onto her own face. She still remembered the bitter taste as she licked her lips. In the knowledge that her father was a perverted murderer and she had attacked him, her fear was indescribable. Supreme.

However she felt no guilt, only terror. He now controlled her. His threat ever etched into her brain and into her heart.

"I will do to you what you did to me, and you *KNOW I WILL DO IT – AND WORSE!"*

And he would.

So as time went by he continued controlling her, making her so fearful he insisted she had to carry out his dirty perverted deeds after it was impossible for him to do so. He submerged himself in ravishing glory as he listened to the news on the radio reporting on the horrific murders that were taking place and that he was not responsible *this time*. But nonetheless he was indeed still doing them through his daughter. He would never be caught.

"Daddy, I am too tired. I'm so tired, Daddy. Let me go to bed!" Simone insisted.

"I want to taste your latest lover Simone. No need to freeze it, pop it straight into the microwave. That would be quicker and then you can get some beauty sleep, you fucking slag."

With an overwhelming surge of anger, Simone could not take anymore.

Opening the chest freezer she rummaged into the bottom of the large white container and found the largest hand. The rigid twisted form fitted comfortably in her hand as she walked towards her father who continued to hurl profanities at her.

Raising her arms high above her head she began to batter his shiny bald head with the frozen fist screaming hysterically as she rhythmically pulped his head.

"Why didn't I do this to you earlier? You make me do this to others! You make me have blood on my hands! So why I couldn't do this to you until now I don't know! You bastard. You bastard. *You fucking bastard*!"

Blood once again covered her. The lilac linen trouser suit now stained with globules of red and white tissue, looked grotesque and vulgar. Her father's head was now only a bloody pulverised stump. His glasses now crushed at her feet. Simone sobbed into his lap. She now had no one. He had taught her all she knew, but she could no longer kill for *HIS* pleasure.

She was able to detach herself from her clients but all she ever wanted was love. Love from her father, love from a friend. But he had put a stop to everything. Even her mother was murdered by him when she was only eight years old. Her dying face forever seared inside her mind.

It was over. It was time to end it.

Walking up the stairs slowly and with a defeated stance she entered into the kitchen. Reaching for the vodka bottle she downed most of it in one prolonged swig. Tears stung her eyes, her heart ached for all the pain she must have caused others, and that of her father. Still she felt fear. *So what if she had money? She had nothing else. With no love or self respect, what's the point of having money? What was the point in living?*

Turning on the gas oven, it hissed into life as hers was about to disperse.

This was music to her ears as she knelt down and placed her head into the deep shadowy cavity of the oven. She inhaled deeply for the last time as she drifted off into a peaceful and fearless sleep.

GROWING PAINS

"Mummy, I don't feel well, my chest hurts!" Sammy moaned more urgently as Trinny walked hastily into the bedroom.

"Come on now, the medicine I gave you earlier must be kicking in by now, sweetie." Trinny desperately tried to reassure her five year old son Matty as he continued to writhe in agony within the bedclothes. It was 2am, and Trinny had been visiting Matty regularly due to his constant complaints of a sore chest.

"Do you love me, Mum?" He pleaded.

"Of course I do, why do you ask?"

"Well, me and Will have been learning a song. It's your favourite. That Nat King Cole song *'If I give my heart to you.'*"

Trinny smiled with an air of hesitation. He was right. For ever since the sudden parting of her husband Keith six months ago, Trinny had continually played this track. She did this in the desperate hope to rekindle the good memories of her now broken marriage.

William lay in the top bunk, staring up at the ceiling listening to the conversation below. Will, in his ten years had never felt such bitterness as he did so right now. He resented deeply that his beloved Dad had left him for an up and coming Lawyer, leaving his mum to bring them up alone on a meagre wage.

Worse, he hated Matty for always insisting he felt ill, grabbing his mum's attention constantly. He felt utterly abandoned, he felt rejected by all of those that he cared for.

"Why honey, that's lovely. So are you going to perform the song for me? How much have you learned already?"

"Well, the first two verses anyway," Matty retorted and started to sing the lyrics awkwardly.

'If I give my heart to you, will you handle it with care?'

Will covered his head with his pillow shaking with frenzied fury. Trinny left the room, her heart warming as she kept the door slightly ajar, ready and willing to receive the cries of her younger son.

***

"Pssst, Matty. You know what would make her really happy?" Will whispered, leaning down from his bunk and yanking the covers off Matty.

"No. What?" Matty questioned.

"Well, wait there and I will be back, this would be the best valentine present you could give her."

"What is *it*?" Matty spoke with more urgency.

"Shhh wait there, I will be straight back!"

Will slid off the wooden bunk, left the bedroom and crept into the dimly lit hall. He silently descended the staircase and into the kitchen.

Returning up the stairs with slow and purposeful steps, he carefully hid the object behind his back.

"*She's gonna love this*!" Will whispered to himself as he walked down the corridor that led back to his bedroom.

"Matty, wake up and lie still!"

With such vigour and passion, Matty didn't even stir as Will manically rammed the knife into Matty's sore chest and began to carve out his brother's heart brutally. Blood layered his face as he worked, scarlet liquid gushed over the bed, staining the Power Rangers wallpaper with rich clots of bloody juice. Finally delving into the crevices of his brothers broken body, Will grabbed the pulsing organ in both hands as he dropped the butcher's knife to the floor.

Lifting his blood soaked face he turned to the open door. Will cheerfully, yet slyly called out.

"Mum! Mum, come quick! Matty's chest is still hurting him, but I think I have found the problem!"

TO HAVE AND TO HOLD

A rustle and a thud alerted Abby that the morning post had arrived. She was sipping coffee as she saw the pile of letters lying randomly on her laminated flooring. Scooping up the heap of letters she walked back into the living room and sat on the leather bound sofa that she obsessively kept in pristine condition.

Opening the first letter, she scanned the usual circular telling her how much she could save if she took out a loan. She then ripped it up. As she picked up the second brown letter, a peach coloured envelop caught her eye that lay at the bottom of the pile. Pulling it out, she read the post code. W 7. West London. Inquisitiveness pricked her senses as she urgently pulled her finger under the opening, tearing the envelope fiercely.

'Mr and Mrs William Vokes request the pleasure of your company for the wedding of Jonathan and Sally on the 14th February 2008.'

Abby felt the rise of bitter bile bubble from the depths of her stomach as she read the sickening words that adorned the elaborate scented paper.

"So he's getting married then…To *her*…" Abby spoke out aloud. Sniffing the paper obscenely, she recalled her last day with Jon, the day he told her that their relationship was over, and that he loved someone else.

***

"Abby, I can't live like this; I just don't feel the same way about you anymore, you have changed so much. You smother me, and you never let me live my life. I just can't be imprisoned by your possessiveness any longer."

Jon was sitting with his head in is hands as he desperately broke this shocking news to Abby. Abby actually pitied him. She watched him as tears rolled down his handsome cheek, his strong hands intertwined with each other, shaking delicately. Abby let Jon finish, and then simply turned to him and held him.

She whispered gently, "Jon, we can work this out, I love you, I adore you, that's all. I will let you breath, as long as we are together I will do anything to try and make things right."

"NO!" Jon screamed suddenly. "I want to leave NOW. I can't do this, and I don't love you anymore. There is someone else…"

Abby threw the invitation on the floor. The memory engulfed her like a swamp, drowning her in the smothering mud, choking on the horror of rejection.

"You fucking bastard, I will be at your wedding believe me, *I will be there.*"

***

Abby picked up her keys and slammed her front door shut. Getting into her car, she drove to the Rose and Crown where Sally was having her hen night.

On the passengers seat a black medical bag that housed the tools of her trade, sat snugly against the car seat.

She was an embalmer. She loved her job, and though it was highly depressing for some people to work with the dead, Abby felt a certain solace as she refreshed the faces of those that once held a healthy glow. *The dead can't hurt you* Abby mused; *only those that are alive kill you, inside and out…*

Driving steadily thought the brightly lit London streets, Abby thought about the night ahead. Sally and Abby used to be friends, a long time ago. One could say that they were best friends, up to the point when Abby met and fell for Jon. It was then, that Sally drifted away, presumably jealous of Abby being with a handsome and successful doctor.

After the termination of her relationship, Abby knew the other woman was indeed Sally. Harbouring hatred so severe yet never confronting Sally with her feelings, Abby let the festering loathing build gradually. Though they only saw each other rarely these days, each encounter was polite, albeit awkward, but no animosity was shown, from either side.

Abby never spoke to Sally regarding the break up but on the surface she smiled sweetly though resentfully. The revulsion brewed within her like a fermenting acidic wine. Being at the hen night would be perfect, perfect for the vengeance she sought so urgently and so eagerly.

***

Dressed in a corset, with a bunny girl head dress embellishing her blonde spiral tresses, suspenders and ample makeup, Sally swigged down another vodka. A large L plate labelled her front, promoting her last night as a singleton. Her cheeks glowed, her lipstick askew, nevertheless she looked beautiful. Her petite form was perfectly shaped, her bosom ample but firm. She simply looked radiant, in spite of her crude appearance as a sluttish bunny girl.

Abby touched her own waistline, knowing how similar their bodies looked.

So why did he leave me for her?

Sitting alone, watching Sally guzzle her fifth drink, Abby waited for the time patiently. Presently, Sally noticed Abby sitting alone and left her cackling friends and staggered towards Abby who sat slightly away from the chaotic laughter and the drunken playmates.

"Not joining in for a drink, Abby? Come on, let me buy *YOU* a drink, and let bygones be bygones. I know we were close, but you should be happy for us. I am happy that you are OK with all this. You really are a lot stronger than

Jon made out, but I knew that anyway. I really didn't think you would come tonight, so I guess it's to show me that you accept our marriage?"

Sally giggled childishly, but seemed genuinely sentimental, and eager to talk.

"Yes, Sally, I am here for you tonight. I know how hard it's been for us lately, but it's good to see you happy. Maybe we can rebuild our friendship again, that's why I am here Sally. To start again and to leave the past behind."

Sally hugged Abby hard, a feeling of complete abominate loathing flooded through Abby like a wave of liquefying repugnance.

"Oh Abby, you really have made this the most special of nights, here have my drink, and I will buy you another." With that Sally weaved her way to the bar and bought two large vodka and tonics.

She remembered my favourite drink.

Stumbling back with the drinks, Sally lumbered herself down next to Abby, but was too close for comfort.

"Tell you what, Sally…" Abby shuffled herself away from Sally's perspiring body and continued,

"Seeing it's your big day tomorrow, let me just have this drink, and I will drive you home. You can't be too sizzled the night before you get hitched. You are still at flat B, Sidney Road aren't you?"

"Yes, I am Abby. That's so sweet of you. Guess you drove here then, so that's fine. I will tell Liza not to order the taxi for me then, seeing I have my own chaperone!" Again Sally giggled mindlessly and drowned her last drink.

***

"It's so hard to see in the dark, the lighting in this road has always been so dire." Abby complained in a mocking style.

"Don't be a fuddy-duddy, just take me home, I feel so… SICK. Will you stay and see me in? You can have a coffee if you like, but I just might go straight to bed if that's ok, Abby."

"Ok, just the one." A smirk so faint shadowed across Abby's angelic face, her night was about to begin, and Sally's was about to end.

***

The statuette was clutched desperately in Abby's fist. Anxiety clenched at Abby's gut, twisting and gyrating in her stomach as she raised the figurine above her head and swung with such force against Sally's unsuspecting head that Abby's elbow twisted vulgarly as Sally fell to the floor with a hideous clunk.

Sally's flat was tatty, but neat, and Sally's smashed head lying in the kitchen caused Abby some concern due of the cluttering mess her body made in this tiny kitchenette.

Dragging Sally's body by the hair, she heaved the dead weight onto the fabric sofa, sitting Sally upright. Closing the legs together neatly, she placed the limp arms down by Sally's side. Sally's head lolled to one side, but the left side of her skull was smashed and fractured causing glutinous sticky blood to eject from the wound, streaking her face with rich rusty fluid.

"We need a little talk, Sally," Abby said with an air of haughty arrogance.

"You took Jon away from me. You knew I adored him. We had the perfect life, and you just had to ruin it, didn't you?"

Abby kicked Sally's ankle as she finished the sentence, laddering the stocking leg with the brutal impact.

Looming towards Sally's spiritless body Abby leaned into Sally's perfect face. She licked the drizzling blood from her cheek and smacked her lips together.

"So, your blood tastes this sweet does it? I wonder if Jon ever tasted your insides. Well your pussy maybe, but your blood, that's for me to enjoy."

She continued to lap at the warm blood though it was now cooling on the cheek of Abby's once treasured friend.

Sally's face was now blood free, lapped clean with Abby's busy tongue. Only her hair was tangled with bloody matter, but Abby replaced the wound with the bunny girl head dress. One ear drooped pathetically as Sally sat like a marionette without its strings on the shabby bloodstained sofa.

"Now, for the fun bit. I am going to taste what Jon tastes. *Your little pussy*. I want to see if you keep yourself clean, especially as it's your hen night."

Prising Sally's legs open, and pulling her panties to one side, she delved into the moisture of Sally's opening with her nose and tongue, inhaling her essence and feeling the heat still within the intimate part of Sally's body. The heat emanating from Sally's dead body stirred Abby with a feeling of arousal, so with her right hand, she touched her own personal parts and strummed her vulva frantically. With her other hand, she rammed all four fingers into Sally cleft and urgently pounded the insides. A crescendo of pleasure swept over Abby, and as she reached the pinnacle of her gratification, she stopped the hammering, and lay on the floor, spent.

"Quite a goer aren't you, Sally? No wonder Jon won't let you go. So, tomorrow is the big day, hey? I am going to find your dress. I trust it's in your room somewhere?"

Abby got up, closed Sally's legs and licked the thick creamy fluid from her fingers and straightened her skirt whist walking into the bedroom.

On the bed, the wedding dress lay. Stunning Ivory satin layers of rich fabric gushed over the bed. A tiara with diamonds and pearls lay next to the veil, shimmering in the dim moonlight.

"How quaint," Abby sneered.

Reaching for the tiara she placed it on her head, and turned to the full length mirror that hung behind the door. The image surprised her. How similar she looked to Sally. Abby's blonde hair hung loosely over her ears, though Sally's was curly, but other than that, their body size and shape were almost exact.

Walking out of the pleasant bedroom, Abby returned to the living room. Sally's body now was crooked, her head in one direction, her torso now twisted in another.

Straightening up Sally's slumping body, Abby scolded her.

"You always used to slouch, put your shoulders back and straighten your back. Come on girl, you are getting married in the morning." Abby slapped the cold empty face as she lectured her friend, her enemy, her rival.

As she organised Sally's sagging body, she hummed to herself the wedding tune from My Fair Lady. Satisfied, she stood back and looked at Sally.

Reaching out for her black medical bag that lay on the nearby recliner, she opened the clasp slowly.

Inside her equipment lay neatly in layers of small trays. The eye cap, needle injector, adhesive and wire all lay precisely at the bottom of the tray. Amongst the restoration tools, a scalpel glistened in its sterile glory next to the embalming solution.

Returning to Sally's face, she pulled back all the stray hairs away from the now swelling face. Abby had to work fast. She pulled out a tin from her bag, some sterilising fluid and the scalpel. With a steady hand, and starting from the top left side of Sally's hair line, Abby severed the skin delicately and accurately away from Sally's face, peeling the whole skin very slowly as she carefully carved.

Blood gushed and sapped from the continued cutting, but Abby used a rag to wipe away the mess. Blood drenched every particle of Sally's corset and minuscule clothing. As Sally's face was peeled away, it exposed spongy mushy muscle. All features were totally eradicated, other than two bulbous eyes that were nursed within their muscular sockets. They stared vacantly back at Abby, leaving only a vision of a blood coated cotton wool bud for a head, with eyes as stark as miniature lit light- bulbs.

Dropping the limp skin carefully onto the metal tin, Abby hastily walked into the bathroom with the tray and her surgical bag. As she did so, Sally's body eventually slumped to the floor. The body lay in its own canvas of blood and gore, the bunny rabbit ears now transfused into ruby red.

In the bathroom the light crudely accentuated Abby's lined and hard features. Although she was of fine face, her consuming hatred radiated from every fibre of her being. Her detestation was almost tangible. She smirked at the loose skin that lay pathetically on the silver tray.

"That's my girl." Abby uttered as she reached out for some sterilising fluid and coated her face liberally with the purifying liquid.

After her surgical wash she retrieved the needle, adhesive and wire. Placing the skin across her own face, she stretched the skin to fit the contours of her own face.

What a snug fit.

Miraculously, the skin fitted across her face with ease. Placing her hand over one side of the skin, with her other hand she grabbed the needle that already was threaded with adhesive wiry thread.

Stitching a segment of skin to her own flesh, she secured the outer skin to her hair line. Abby did not flinch with the pain. After smoothing Sally's face over her own, she let the needle hang loosely, and reached for the adhesive glue. She smeared it into her own hairline. The skin stretched into place as Abby manipulated the flesh onto her own. The glue started to set quickly, so Abby had to be exact with the adjustments. With the loose needle, she snipped the thin wire, and secured the other side of her hairline the same way.

Finally, Abby injected a minute amount of embalming fluid into each temple. Flinching from the pain as the needle hit her vein, Abby clenched her teeth in agony. After this, the deed was done. The malleable skin coated Abby's face easily. She stared at her handiwork, and laughed out loud.

"Here's looking at you kid!" Abby hissed with mirth as she left the bathroom and returned to the bedroom.

Here she undressed out of her skirt and blouse that was now stained with Sally's and her own drying blood. Abby then reached for the bridal gown that flaunted the bed. Slipping into the cool fabric, she thrilled at the feel of the satin against her skin, but one other thought captivated her more. It was that of Jon's strong hands caressing her face once more, and her seeing Jon Vokes witnessing her ultimate revenge.

Studying her image in the mirror, she altered a few adjustments to her dress and veil then examined the face once more. In her eyes she looked stunning.

Just as Sally always did.

In her eyes she *was* Sally, and she was going to marry the love of her life tomorrow. Throwing her arms in the air gleefully, she waltzed round the room singing *'The First Cut Is The Deepest'* with the imaginary presence of Jon wrapped within her arms. Blood dripped from her surgical stitching onto the ivory satin, draping the dress with splashes of vibrant scarlet blushes. Abby looked and felt like a queen; tomorrow she would see the love of her life once more.

***

Jon glanced at his watch.

The church was full. A subtle drone of babble filled the pews. The fragrant flowers filled his nostrils with expectation, and awe. He was nervous.

He knew somewhere Abby would be in the congregation, angry that his father had invited her. Nonetheless, this fear was overshadowed with the love and eagerness to marry sweet gentle Sally. His stomach flipped as he turned to his best man to confirm the possession of the ring.

The music changed to *their* song. Eric Clapton's *'Wonderful Tonight'* echoed throughout the church. His bride was here, and he was going to be the happiest man alive. His heart thumped nervously. He was too excited to look behind, wanting to savour the moment of anticipation until he witnesses his bride walk down the aisle; however he didn't want to miss a thing. Gasps filtered out from the congregation as his wife to be walked proudly towards him.

Turning slowly to witness his love, he was shocked to see that she walked down the aisle alone. *Where was Sally's father?* Maybe he was taken ill, but the important thing was that Sally was here, parading down the aisle in all her beauty.

His bride's veil concealed her face, masking her genuine loveliness. But everyone knew how staggeringly beautiful Sally was. Eventually, in perfect timing as the song finished, his bride finally stood side by side next to Jon.

The vicar began to speak.

"Dearly beloved. We are gathered here today to witness the joining of this man and this woman in holy matrimony…" The vicar continued his speech.

Jon felt ecstatic, proud. He was in the throes of *total* happiness as he reached for the veil and pulled up the netted fabric away from Sally's face.

What greeted him left him transfixed. He finally screamed.

The vision before him filled him with such repulsion that Jon nearly vomited. Sally's features had collapsed, sagged. Her beautiful face was blood soaked and shrunken. Her lips were merely a slash. The sneering unspeakable face of Sally filled Jon with such abhorrence that he yelled aggressively;

"Sally? This isn't Sally! *WHERE IS SALLY?*"

"I *am* here my love. Kiss me Jon!" Abby hissed.

As Jon was about to run from the church that was humming with the constant chatter of anxious guests, Abby grabbed Jon and kissed him hard on the month; biting into his bottom lip with such force the rubbery muscle ripped from his mouth instantly.

"To have and to hold, from this day forth, for richer, for poor, in sickness and in health…" Abby continued her marital patter as she heartily masticated on the rest of Jon's lip.

Jon bled profusely, he held the remains of his mouth as the blood spluttered over the vicar and his best man, with pain so agonising he soon realised *who* the impostor was.

"*ABBY?*"

In a desperate need to know the truth, he lurched at her face and as his fingers touched the flexible skin, he tore away the pliable membrane to reveal the true identity.

"Hello, Jon. At last we are together. I simply adore you. You know that don't you? I thought you would be proud of me. I knew we would be together. Sally is in a better place now; she is still a stunning beauty even without her face. But if I can't have you, no one can…"

Jon eventually collapsed as Abby walked towards the altar. Reaching for the gold crucifix that stood prominently and proudly on the intricate altar, Abby grabbed it with both hands and smashed it into Jon's skull as he weakly tried to get up after his fall.

"This is how she died; now you suffer the same fate!"

Abby continued to pulverise Jon's head, more blood and fragmented matter adorning and layering the surrounding guests.

"I love you Jon, now we *can* at last be together forever, you can't rid me that easily, but in death, we can *BE* together!" Abby hysterically screamed.

Reaching for the scalpel that she concealed within her lacy garter, with one clean sweep she swiped at her throat; the blade sinking into her jugular vein effortlessly.

Visceral blood spewed from the clean open wound. She fell freely to the sacred ground.

Together, both bodies lay in a unity of bloody demolition, the congregation now hushed in a state of complete denial and shock. The vicar stood stunned rooted to the spot, his robes stained with the carnage that lay in front of him.

Abby's was at last reunited. Abby's spirit descended into her own welcoming oblivion, knowing that she had achieved her own personal accolade.

DON'T LOOK DOWN

The moon cut through the darkness with its milky shaft of light. Lewis strained his eyes into the glow as this was his only point of consolation. The large beech tree scraped against the window with twisted branches luring him to look, but Lewis was too afraid. His youthful mind taunted him with the notion that *IT* was under the bed. His eyes were focused straight ahead, never daring to turn his head either way.

Every muscle in his body twitched with anticipation from the imminent manifestation of the bogeyman to slide from below and to grab him down to the cavern of hell where it dwelled. Turning his eyes to the window, the tree had finally won. Lewis focused his weary eyes onto the gnarled branches that rhythmically and relentlessly scratched the glass surface. Dark silhouettes of beguiling arms reached out beseeching with Lewis to *not* look under the bed.

"*Stay with us…*" The wind and branches whispered to him with hypnotic tones, caressing him away from looking below. The wind with a crescendo of caution travelled and embraced the building, comforting its inhabitants.

"Shhh…!" Lewis reluctantly retorted as the sound became amplified inside his cluttered head.

His mind wandered. He recalled the moment the pencil ground into the soft vulnerable flesh, the pale neck vomiting burgundy fluid. With pleading eyes bulging with intense incredulity, a quiver of a lip, a fruitless lift of a wavering arm, and it was all over. So quick, so final. No child should *see* such a pitiful death.

Though Lewis was now sixteen years of age, he still needed a comforting hand to stroke his clammy brow. The bogeyman continued to terrify him, just as it did when he was of such a tender age. Rancid hands would slowly secrete and slither from under the valance. Rusty substance oozed from behind the sharpened fingernails, as they wormed their spindly bony arms around Lewis's panting and heaving body. Finally they would crush his neck until he no longer had the breath to scream, or even to weep.

Lewis would wake within the damp moist sheets, perspiration budding from under his hairline. His body throbbed with panic; nevertheless he was relieved it was only a nightmare. His brother in the next bed often brought him back to reality with his irritable, "What the hell Lewis, shut the fuck up!" bawl.

However every night the thought of the bogeyman plagued him, teasing and testing his conscious and subconscious mind.

But at this moment it was paramount. As of tonight the unremitting hellish visions were about to reach its final climax. A conclusion. Struggling against his will to look under the bed and that of the comforting tree with its lullaby of calm, Lewis managed to force his stiff body with laboured exertion, to look down. He had never done this before. Fear had always paralysed him, but in order to end these horrific nightmares tonight he was compelled to look.

The rustle of his duvet interrupted the cooing wind as he leaned over his bed. Squeezing his eyes securely shut, he could see a myriad of floating abstract tinted images darting and waltzing within his head. His chestnut hair flopped to the floor; hands gripping the edge of the metal bed. Lewis eventually opened his eyes.

His mother's decomposing body lay still, silent, her eyes staring into the coils of his mattress. The pencil still jarred into her bloodless neck.

From her unyielding mouth echoic words uttered repeatedly;

"It's you. You *are* the bogeyman Lewis. *You*. Look what you did to me!"

Lewis with frantic hands muffled his ears and screamed. Disorientation engulfed him.

The nurse heard his maniacal cries. With a syringe by her side she strode down the whitewashed corridor and entered his stark sterile room, as she did almost every night.

FIRST IMPRESSION

He sipped his tepid drink in the shadowy darkness. Random flashes of coloured light illuminated his face, accentuating his dark brooding eyes and aquiline nose. Though not handsome, the man was exceptionally striking; his black undulating hair hung loosely around his face framing his classic features.

The music pulsed throughout his body causing his ears to pound with the monotonous thud of a heavy booming bass. This didn't bother him, he was here to watch and absorb the sensual female as she gyrated erotically on the slippery dance floor. Sweat, stains from previously spilt drinks and gum littered the ground, but miraculously she held her position and stole the show. She shone. By god she shone.

The other dancers on the tacky floor had faded into obscurity. His groin ached for her, throbbed in time with the music as she opened her legs and rhythmically rocked her body to the music. The black halter neck top that was adorned with coloured sequins held her upper body snugly, her breasts swelling over the neck line statuesquely. Two large mounds rose and fell beneath the material as she seductively bounced them in unison with the music.

She returned his gaze a few times, her dark eyes teasingly testing him, causing him to sweat and tingle insatiably with the oozing energy she conjured, that in turn created an energy of his own that was private and forbidden. Eventually the salty sting from his penetrative stare finally caused him to blink.

As he did so, the enchanting woman turned on her heel and walked seductively up to him, grinning with an air of mischief.

"Well, well, well, we are having a good old gawk aren't we, huh? Do I do it for you?" Gina slung her head back with a derisory laugh. After being over zealous with the margaritas, Gina's confidence was soaring. How she loved the attention. Her dampened strands of bleached blonde hair wormed around her flushed cheek, coils of hair dripping in sweat as it glistened and slithered down her slender neck.

He finally spoke.

"You are gorgeous. There is something about you. I want to paint you." Gina sniggered childishly as she slumped next to him onto the smoke fumed sofa, grabbing a bottle and greedily downed the final dregs of lukewarm beer.

"You what?" she spluttered as she swallowed the last of the liquid.

"You some kind of artist then?" Gina's interest grew.

"Yes, and I do portraits, they sell for a good price, I think you would be a good subject." His smile captivated Gina. In spite of her tipsy state, she was drawn into his sapphire blue eyes as his lively yet direct stare engrossed her.

"If you painted me, what would I get out of it? I mean would you pay *me?*"

"I would pay you, yes. In any manner you wish." He took her hand delicately that was bejewelled with bangles and rings. Charmingly, he kissed her knuckles, his eyes locking into her.

***

"My studio is on the top floor."

He wrapped his arm around Gina protectively as she felt the pinching icy wind prick at her body. She shuddered from the cold but also from the chemistry that secreted from her handsome stranger. He was the perfect gentleman and with his exceeding good looks he indeed looked like a priceless work of art.

They walked towards the large old warehouse that had now been converted into apartment blocks. Large and austere windows gazed down at her, some with a welcoming warm amber light, but others cold and calculating, empty and abandoned.

Together they entered the large lobby doors, where a vast entrance hall greeted them. In the dimly lit hallway, shadows fell upon a row of closed doors on either side with gold plated numbers adorning the wooden doors. On her left as she walked beside her 'Prince Charming', a large caged lift was the essential feature to the foyer.

Hand in hand, they silently walked towards the enormous metal lift. Their footsteps pronounced as they walked along the marbled floor. Arriving at the ancient monstrosity, Isaac drew back the rusty metal gate that enclosed the shaft. They stepped into the empty enclosure. Their pending passion held in divine anticipation. He finally jabbed the worn out button. Boring into Gina's thirsty eyes Isaac suddenly turned. Pulling her towards him he kissed her hard on the mouth. The lift jerked into life as it ascended. Its echoic mechanical drone reverberated, consuming the building, as did the sound of their breathless desperate kisses.

Their mouths never parted. Arms explored each other's bodies in frantic lust. Moans of ecstasy filled the metal cubicle as it roared up towards the dwelling where their lovemaking would eventually reach a climax. The ramifications of Gina's actions never entered her mind.

***

"So, what is your name?" Gina asked as she covered herself in the warm damp sheet as she slid off the bed, their musty scent still evident. Walking towards the elaborate arched window which allowed the creamy moonlight to illuminate the room, her form was silhouetted as she stood and stared out of the window.

"Isaac. And I know you are Gina. I have often seen you with your sister dancing at 'The Tube'; you have gained quite a name for yourself."

She turned around, a smile developing upon her sun kissed face. She walked back towards him; the sheet falling to the floor revealing her glistening marblesque body.

"*Isaac*. How sophisticated, very fitting for an artist!"

She slid back onto the bed, mounting her new found lover. Her blonde locks fell against her face, framing her features perfectly in the moonlight.

"This is how I want to remember you, Gina." Isaac retorted.

"I want this moment to remain with me for ever." Carefully lifting her from his torso, he kissed her nose as she fell onto her back, her matted hair wild and scattered against the pillow. Slinking out of the bed he slowly walked towards a room that was adjacent to the kitchenette. The door was made of solid steel and to confirm Gina's enquiring expression, with a sibilant tone he whispered;

"The old safe room, Gina." Blowing her a kiss, he disappeared through the heavy strengthened doors.

Gina surveyed the vast room in his absence. In spite of the shadows that cast an ominous light, Gina noticed an abundance of houseplants, canvases, easels and colour splattered work benches. Low beams hung overhead, pinned with jumbled newspaper clippings, sketches and photographs.

I can't believe he is going to paint me now she mused as Isaac returned. He was clutching some paint brushes and a large white canvas. His lean naked body still held evidence of his arousal.

Ruffling her hair she sat up.

"In the darkness, I am going to create a masterpiece. Come. Come lie with me here on the chaise lounge and I will sketch your perfection upon this blank canvas."

Gina was intrigued with his manner. He was so precise with everything he said, albeit limited. His lovemaking made up for his restricted speech. He pointed into the shadows, beckoning her to follow. She obediently did as she was told and followed him to the other side of the studio.

Several times Isaac stopped momentarily, gazing at her with longing, or was it love? Gina's insides flipped as his eyes once again stimulated feelings that have never be awakened before. Isaac slipped behind a pair of elaborate embroidered curtains, the material wafted air into Gina's face as he disappeared between the folding fabric. Still naked, Gina spilt the curtains apart, the moonlight unable to penetrate the dark dense area that greeted her.

"Isaac? Isaac, where are you?" She tripped over a metallic tin, the sound rattling though the air with a harsh clatter.

"Isaac! I can't see you. Where the hell are you?"

"Gina. I am waiting for you, look for me."

The sound of a lit match cut into the quietness, sulphur and candle wax invaded her senses. A flickering tawny light filtered the generously spaced but murky room.

Almost immediately Gina could see a beautifully crafted oak carved chaise-lounge, graced in deep burgundy velvet. Isaac stood behind the stunning recliner, his hand in an open gesture for her to lie down.

"Come lie for me, my beauty." Isaac took her arm as Gina keenly obliged. The rest of the room was shrouded in candle light as Isaac started to caress her supple naked body.

"I will soon begin. But first, my beauty I want you to relax. Focus on me, as I create you into an exquisite unique creation."

Moving to the already erected canvas that stood regally on its stand, Isaac started to pleasure himself as Gina wriggled around on the chaise-lounge invitingly, then finally finding a comfortable position, she lay still.

Feeling deeply aroused herself she watched her lover handle himself. After only a short moment, he stepped behind his canvas, and with frantic waves from his charcoal pencil he started to sketch the fundamental contours of her shape. He paused after a few moments.

"Gina, let me take a break, just for a moment. I would be happy to offer you some wine. Look, come and view what I have already done!"

Gina rose from her base and walked towards Isaac. His extraordinary features shadowed in the ochre glow that radiated around the room. Gina observed the image in front of her. She was overwhelmed at the perfect creation that adorned the fabric. The dark charcoal had outlined each feature exactly; even the small lines under her neck were visible.

"Isaac, this is *me*, it's simply perfect."

Handing Gina some rosé wine, Isaac returned the compliment.

"I am glad you approve. But now Gina, we need colour! I have outlined you as I see you. Now wait for the colour and you will see yourself come alive."

Sipping her wine, Gina was in awe. How he fashioned such detail in such a small period of time astounded her.

"Finish your wine and then recline." Isaac smiled at his subject relishing in his witty poetic sentence. Gina blushed as she guzzled the acidic but welcoming fluid.

Gina nestled against the warm smooth velvet, her eyes becoming heavy as she focused on her lover. Her mind swirling, Gina became alarmed at how much she must have drunk throughout the night, surely she should not be feeling this woozy after all the time that had lapsed since her last drink. With that notion, Gina fell into a deep, blissful but sudden sleep.

***

She awoke with a start, as the blade delicately and finely sliced into the surface of her abdomen. The room was lit so brightly she felt as though she was in hospital. No such luck. She saw Isaac still naked wearing a surgical mask. He stooped over her, focused in absolute concentration as he carefully portioned a fine segment from her tanned belly. The pain engulfed her, the cold sharp steel of the scalpel carving into her skin with ease as knife into butter. No scream came. Only the intense pain and fear surrounded her as she fell into a chasm of searing pain and terror. Gina wriggled her upper body in defence. Alerted that she was finally awake, Isaac stopped carving.

"See, here we have the richness I am trying to create. Your blood will be the base colour of my creation and I will use parts of your skin and body to give emphasis of texture to create the most perfect mosaic effect. Now don't be alarmed, my love. I only need your eye lids to capture your rapturous beauty - for the moment." A glass beaker was half full of crimson liquid, a catheter still hanging from inside.

Gina again unable to respond to the monstrous statement fruitlessly tried to struggle, however her legs rooted to the spot. Noticing the equipment set up in front of her, she realised that part of her body was under some type of anaesthetic. Even though she could not feel her legs, she could feel the searing pain as the scalpel started to peel away the upper layer of her eye lid, blood dripping into her eye as the skin peeled away with ease. Her sight blurred as blood filtered into her reducing vision. Isaac grasped the tiny piece of skin and started to manipulate the malleable material, stretching it into the correct shape for his 'masterpiece.' Glancing at his lover that had now become his victim, he smiled as he positioned the piece of skin around the charcoaled outline of her smouldering eyes.

"Now, for my favourite part."

He leaned closer, stroking and fondling her breast before he sliced the surface of skin from the tender innocent swelling. Pain coursed through her body, lightning flashed before her blood tainted eyes as the unforgiving agony swamped her being. Layering the cut skin onto the canvas, he unwittingly placed the scalpel against her firm but damaged stomach as he reached for the necessary adhesive. Gina, though partially paralysed and in spite of her unrelenting suffering, impulsively grabbed the surgical tool in her weakening hand, then delved the sharp weapon furiously into his femoral artery. Blood leaked from his groin, rustic fluid spewing from the lethal wound. Isaac turned to her. With a paling face that was etched in disappointment, he slumped against her stomach.

"What have you done?" he stammered.

"You have ruined my creation. *Our creation*. Gina, this would have been so perfect for my collection..." With a stilted sob, Isaac ungainly fell to the ground as he tried to raise his head ineffectively. Clutching his bleeding wound in desperation, his final words circulated through Gina's fading mind.

"Go, see. You will see my Darlings, they are all around me. I have never been alone, Gina. Until now. They are my creations of natural life. They live, Gina, they still live, in *me*..."

As he died, Gina indeed continued to live. After a couple of hours of staring at the stiffening body that lay beside her and the heavily artexed ceiling where horrifying twisted images formed from the undulating creases, she eventually regained feeling in her heavy legs and dragged herself off her back.

With her legs now gaining stability, she still felt paralyzed with fear. Her naked body dripped in blood streaking her skin in a ruby river of tears. Turning her back to the pathetic heap that lay redundant on the floor, she tore the decorative curtain from its wooden rings and wrapped it around her cut and peeling body.

Only now could she cry. Her body racked in pain as each sob shook her spoilt quivering frame.

Looking around the studio she noticed the photos and the clippings once more. Approaching them, she analysed the pictures. Her eyes fell on beautiful women, carefree full of life. Photos of the living, but pictures of the dead lay nearby she feared.

***

She walked towards the room that Isaac previously had wandered into after their sensational lovemaking. Her heart hardened at the very memory of his touch. Unbolting the heavily bolted steel door, she entered the room. Gina was greeted by an odorous stench. Here she had found his 'Darlings'. Their bodies piled up in a mountain of decomposing flesh.

Their hideous portraits were elevated above the stack of skeletal bodies, erected on steel girders high and majestic, looking down on the pathetic waste of what was once human life. Their life. Oh such bitter portraits, their eyes watching her as she witnessed the slaughtered corpses.

Repulsed, Gina left the doorway to hell and hobbled towards the still lit candle that twinkled desperately; desperate to hold onto its last embers. Using the curtain that embraced her ruined body she set it alight. Reaching for the shirt that Isaac had originally worn, Gina placed it upon her bleeding body, crying out as the fabric touched her seeping wounds. She shuddered with the thought that his body once filled these sleeves. Finding her jeans, she arduously stepped into them, sobbing through her uncontrollable pain. Picking up her handbag, she left the apartment sizzling, as portraits and furniture went up in a blaze.

As the lift descended to the ground floor, she knew the occupant lying on the top floor would be descending into his well deserved hell. She heard the hiss as fire engulfed the carnage that had lay undiscovered for so long.

"Come die for me, you bastard!" Gina muttered to herself as she limped out of the building and called herself an ambulance.

***

He was charismatic. She surveyed his physique as he leant against the bar. The wine glass clutched within her shaking hand was almost empty. Her burdened expression was hidden behind a baseball cap. Fleetwood Mac's 'Big Love' surrounded the nightclub, the words pulsing inside her head.

'*Looking out for love…*'

And indeed she was. She longed to feel the touch of a loving hand, a tender kiss from someone that cherished her for who she was now. Her focus was on the young man that was slowly becoming an obsession; she needed to feel treasured again. Her scarred face and body had long since prohibited her from ever dancing again, let alone relish in the knowledge that she could seduce a man with a wink of an eye, or a swagger from her hips.

Watching the young man wave to his friends that were larking about on the dance floor, he reluctantly joined them, leaving his soda on the side of the bar. He was obviously the taxi service for the night. Sliding anonymously to where he had stood, she nodded to the barman to tend to her requirements.

"One large white wine and whatever he had. Soda was it?" Gina nodded toward the young man that was joining his jovial friends.

"Yup Gina, it was. He had loads of ice. Do you want me to add a little extra? It could be your lucky night."

"Don, you are a star, if you could. I owe you one. I know how you like it when I give you head."

With a false smutty smile, Gina licked her lips vulgarly.

Don touched himself behind the counter envisaging his impending gratification. After winking at Gina he attended to the drinks, adding only a few drops of Rohypnol to the heavily iced soda.

Gina remained at the bar waiting for her man to return and to drain his drink after his exertion on the dance floor. Watching from behind the peak of her cap, the handsome man eventually returned to the bar exhausted from his laboured dancing, he had no rhythm at all. No matter. He was thirsty and as predicted he swallowed his soda in one mouthful.

"Hey, who filled this up?" He noticed after putting his glass down.

"I did, I bought you a drink. You looked as though you needed some hydration!"

Gina answered in her most sultry of voices. Her long glossy blonde curls poured around her face hiding her imperfections. She subtly turned her ruined side away from him.

In the dimness of the nightclub, the young man looked at her, and smiled.

"Why thanks, aren't you a pretty one?"

Smiling bashfully she bit on her bottom lip suggestively.

"You wanna come back with me? I can show you a good time handsome."

As she finished her sentence, he began to feel a strange sensation travel through him. Warmness enveloped his body as his legs lost their stability and his arms felt heavy.

"God, it's hot in here, I need to fucking lie down." He stuttered.

"I live next door, come with me and I will take care of you. Come on, I need a man close to me tonight..." Gina invited.

Calling out to his friends in slurred speech as they still fooled around on the grimy dance floor, he coarsely yelled;

"Get your own lift back folks, I've pulled!"

Purposefully Gina grabbed him and dragged the staggering man behind her, as he desperately tried to grope her perky behind.

***

Ramming the key into the lock, a feeling of wellbeing overwhelmed her, as the perfect victim was about to become *part* of her. His skin would fit snugly against her own. At last she would feel the heat from a real man again. She would dress herself up in his skin and eventually she would be feeding her uncontrollable lust for male contact and revenge.

"Come lie for me, I will give you rest, you can sleep for as long as you want, my beauty." Her voice was smooth, engaging. Turning away from the shadows, she removed her cap revealing her hideously scarred eye; her gaze channelling into the young man's addled brain. His scream was muted as he fell into the opening doorway. The door closed, leaving the fading beat of the nightclub behind them.

THE LETTER

Sandwark Prison 1953

Letter found in cell 298 after the execution of Mr. James Garwin.

Dear Mother,					2nd July 1953 10.20am

    Within these tatty sheets I want to explain, if I may, why I am sitting in this barren cell awaiting execution. I want to first point out to you the reasons why I did, and would have continued with these acts that I enjoy, if I had not had the misfortune of being caught by a vigilant member of the public. I am not a monster, mother. I am a human being, though there are many who I know wish me dead, and indeed my execution is ever looming as I pen each syllable to you at this moment.

    I have one more hour left to tell you mother, about how I feel, along with a deserving explanation. On a positive note, it seems that I have become a celebrity, so now at last you can be proud of me, mother.

    I want you to know how my mind works and how things affect me. So let me start by telling you how I felt when I first came into contact with my first victim back in 1933. At twenty three years of age, I eventually fled your suffocating nest. Oh, the freedom was great mother. Liberating, fulfilling, but still I needed more. So much more.

    Tina Ainswoth. My, she was a beauty. She moved me. My groin would twitch urgently as I watched her leave her tiny floral cottage where she lived and slept. At nineteen she radiated a heat within me that scorched my mind. My body would quiver and I would have to swallow the floods of saliva that filled my mouth. She looked delicious. Yes, I could have eaten her there and then.

Anyway, I digress.

As she walked down the footpath towards the village church, I stood behind a gravestone surveying her as she entered the cool dark doors for her pending choir practise. The peeling bells melodically weaved their hopeful invitation to those that were drawn to the cloisters of the church to redeem their sins.

Not I.

I, on the other hand have no conscience at all, hence my confinement within these stifling walls. I watched her enter the foreboding building. The need to delve into the sacred area of this young goddess, which teased my poisonous mind and body with her sexual enticement, absorbed me. I am a simple unassuming man, with needs. However, my certain needs can be overwhelming, to me and for my lovers. She never knew my love for her was so abundant. She didn't even know who I was until I eventually had her as my possession, but I will tell you presently how I achieved such a task, so easily.

I continued to lurk outside the church, waiting. The muffled choral hymns did little to sanctify me. The organ droned majestically as lyrical voices eager to praise their god sang with desperation so paramount, I laughed.

'THERE IS NO BLOODY GOD. YOU ARE DOING THIS PURELY BECAUSE YOU ARE SCARED OF DYING. YOU ARE ONLY TERRIFIED OF THE ETERNITY OF EMPTINESS THAT GREETS YOU WHEN YOU DIE!' I recall hissing these words out loud from behind an old headstone, as memoires of my regimented religious upbringing caused me to seethe in anger.

How could there be a God when the punishments you implemented were so severe. Alone I would hide from your thudding rhythmic steps as you clutched the whip in your vein channelled hand. Huddled and naked, I would hide in the coal shed, but you always found me and your punishment would begin. My screams never stopped your beatings; the clumps of my blonde hair grasped in your spindly hands never caused you to cease, but only made you continue more as you cursed me for looking untidy and dirty as black streaky tears fell down my smudged face.

Ironically, you did look awfully dishevelled mother. After you had your way with me, your mousey hair always managed to come unpinned, you looked exhausted also. Ugly dare I say? I understand now, it was all for my own good.

Look at me now. You have done well, mother. The perfect son. Am I not?

I will continue about my love and longing for Tina. Once again I have gone off on a tangent.

I had such deep desires to explore. The insatiable need to search and touch Tina's exotic forbidden fruit consumed me. She was the serpent, I was mankind. After her choir practise I watched as she exited the church, her raven hair curled fashionably under her collar with hair pins clasping at her temples. I removed myself from the damp stones and followed her. To my utter horror Tom Green met her at the edge of the footpath and they embraced. Mother, the anger was supreme. You must have felt this brand of anger, as I often saw this in your eyes when you bashed my head against the cold walls of our delightful home.

Then I had a plan.

As they walked along the footpath that merged into a rapeseed field that was in full bloom, I left the graveyard and walked towards her tiny cottage. Her back window had been left open; I had noticed this earlier as I watched her that morning. It was this moment that I felt a huge surge of power. I suddenly felt in control. Mother, I had made a decision and it was at this crucial moment that determined who I am today.

Her house was untidy surprisingly; I noticed dirty plates in the sink as I lowered myself onto the cluttered worktop of her tiny kitchen. The window was a tight squeeze, but being the slender snake that I am, I slithered in silently. She had eaten some bread and jam; I noticed this as my hand smudged against the burgundy sticky gel.

Leaving the cluttered kitchen, I ascended the tiny cottage stairs. Sweet quaint pictures of young children fishing shrouded the whitewashed walls. I found her room straight away, as there were only two rooms once I reached the top of the staircase.

Again her room was untidy, but comfortable. Dirty laundry was scattered around the wicker basket; she must have thrown them in and missed. I found this endearing. Picking up some panties, I inhaled her musty essence. This was the closest I got to her sacred fruit and later I would indeed be having so much more.

As my anticipation pricked me, I found her wardrobe. The perfect hiding place. I edged myself between the empty hangers, floral dresses, hat boxes and a camel coat. Her shoes lay at my feet. The stale smell of sweat from her shoes filled my nostrils, oh how I loved her odour. Still with her used panties in my hand, I stood within the dark dank closet continually inhaling her fragrance so I didn't feel so alone.

I waited. Silence throbbed around me. I was like a snake about to pounce on a rodent, I was rigid with expectancy.

Thoughts of you interrupted my concentration.

Mother, as I waited in baited breath for my lover, images of *your* love came to me in horrific flashes. However appalling they were, I embraced them.

Your face contorted with aggression as you stripped me and poked artefacts inside my tender areas. Your smiles seemed to be misplaced considering the injuries you were inflicting upon me. But now as a forty-three year old man waiting to be hanged, I see why you laughed and smiled as you dealt with me so ruthlessly.

Again, I deviate.

She arrived.

In spite of having no belief in God, I found myself thanking him. She was alone. Through the tiny eyehole I watched her throw her clutch bag onto the bed. She then threw herself onto the thick scarlet bed spread, her ebony hair cresting around her perfect features.

My groin once again bulged, almost to the point of pain as I continued to watch her lie on the bed holding up a flower and a small bottle of fragrance in front of her radiant face. *She looked so happy.* These items must have been a gift from Mr Tom Green who worked as a clerk in the nearby town.

It was time.

My body and mind could no longer hold in that urgent need. I had for her.

She screamed as I stepped out of the wardrobe, my smile didn't comfort her at all. She instinctively sat up and resorted to a defensive posture, shielding her body with her knees. Her stocking legs looked soft and silky, but I needed to feel the flesh that lay behind the tantalising fabric. I pushed her down forcefully and cooed to her to be silent. I was surprised at my own strength. She fought like a young deer, her gangly legs hitting out at me in a frantic panic.

With my left arm I held her down firmly by her throat and with my right arm I ripped the stocking off one of her thrashing legs.

Balling the warm stretchy fabric in my hand, I rammed it into her mouth, her screams now muffled perfectly as she gagged into the moistening textile. Now with both hands, I pinned her down and I discussed with her what I had planned. After my direction she finally quietened. Tears rolled down her flushed cheeks like drops of fresh dew falling from a rose at the break of dawn.

I placed my hand under her tweed skirt, feeling the soft supple flesh of her inviting cavity. Sweeping up her skirt and jarring her legs into the air, I saw her oasis of desire. She wore no panties.

Her opening flourished before me like a soft pink orchid, teasing me to enter. Mother, I have to explain that it was at this point the anger appeared. I felt a huge sense of rage as I thought about Tom Green and how he must have searched her delights before I did.

She was stained. With such force my desire turned to hate, my love for her was no more. Letting her legs drop to the bed I began to pound and hit her stomach, face and her groin. With each blow she became more submissive.

I grabbed the stocking out of her mouth and unravelled it as I continued to punch her with my other fist. Her face then turned a shade of slate grey as I wrapped the stocking around her tiny neck and garrotted her, and as I pulled the fabric tighter, her face distorting in colour and in shape, I saw you. It was your face looking back at me, your face I was killing. I felt such elation!

Did I eventually feel the power and control that you experienced when you punished me, Mother?

After my hatred for Tina subsided I felt love once more. Her body now still and warm, I knew this was the right time. I made love to Tina. My first time, mother! It was the most exquisite feeling that I had ever experienced, such a shame I had not felt this love before, it seemed so real and mother, it *was* real.

We were lovers. Slowly and lovingly we made sweet music, her body still flaccid and supple as I planted my seed into my sweet Tina. The implications of my actions never entered my mind as I plunged myself inside her.

I slipped out of her, leaving my Ophelia floating down the petal filled stream. My goddess, my sweet love.

After my first experience with Tina who I will still miss, until the moment my feet dangle and twitch from under the gallows, I knew this was the road to gratification. I had a feeling of accomplishment, even a feeling of belonging. I was always clever, if not devious at concealing my actions and as a young man that soon became respected within Caters Solicitors, no one ever suspected me.

I never felt alone when I was with my lovers; they showed me so much love once I had slaughtered them. I will be perfectly honest, the slaughtering got extremely messy, but I also found great satisfaction when I submerged myself within their pools of scarlet warmth. You would have been so angry if you found out how dirty I got. Back to the coal shed you would have banished me, I wouldn't be surprised! I am laughing now as I write this, as I have about fifteen minutes until I take my last breath.

I have to pause mother. A priest has just come into my cell and blessed me. He read out the Lord's Prayer to me.

"…and lead us not into temptation deliver us from evil…"

Bit late for that I must say.

He left me the bible as he departed.

I just picked up the leather bond book, flicking through the pages. A passage within the fine limp sheets did make me smile.

Here, I will jot them down for you.

"There are six things the LORD hates, seven that are detestable to him: haughty eyes, a lying tongue, hands that shed innocent blood, a heart that devises wicked schemes, feet that are quick to rush into evil, a false witness who pours out lies and a man who stirs up dissension among brothers."

Mother, I don't think I will be welcomed into the Kingdom of Heaven do you?

I have about five minutes left. Fear is now sweeping and swelling within me. Like an angry sea my fear is drowning me. I am questioning death for the first time. As the biblical passage quotes, there will be no heaven for me, but I knew that anyway. I fear the blackness and the abyss of nothingness that I will fall into once my last breath is taken. But mother, I took life from my lovers. Now they take my life from me. They must have feared death too, but I feel they must have feared me more...

Mother, my cell is opening. The heavy slide of metal and the clinking of the heavy keys have alerted me it's time.

The priest has returned and goodness how elegantly he stands before me. He is watching me write my very last words, his eyes are black like the devil himself. I can hear more shuffling from outside my cell. Steady footsteps are coming down the dismal passageway to take me to my awaiting death. Five men are here, their faces are grave. I wonder what my grave will look like. Will you be laying flowers on the freshly laid earth? They are urging me to close, so I will write my last sentence to you mother. I write in haste now.

They will be leading me down the corridor in silence I imagine, as the priest may well chant some prayer in hope I will be received into the Kingdom of God. If God can't forgive me, I doubt you ever could.

One last thing, Mummy, will it hurt?

Yours in oblivion,

Your son, James

A TASTE OF YOUR OWN MEDICINE

Jake swiftly pulled on his police jacket as he exited his flat. Slamming the front door firmly behind him, he double checked that it was secure. He couldn't be too careful; this block of flats was notorious for thieves and addicts who leapt at any opportunity to force themselves into poorly secured properties.

After successfully completing his probation as a trainee constable, Jake appreciated his time at his new appointed headquarters. Having been a police officer for only a few months now, Jake was happy with his routine every morning, in spite of the dubious area in which he lived.

Leaping down the flight of concrete graffiti riddled steps two at a time; he felt a tinge of excitement. Today he was having his appraisal, and he knew he would be rewarded in some way for his thorough and committed work. After living in this run down English town for most of his life, Jake was determined to work for the police force. He felt someone had to try and protect those residents that tried to earn a decent and honest living.

His father had been one of them, but he had been brutally stabbed as he waited for the number 83 bus. Tom Staples had been eliminated with a single thrust; he died instantly and alone. The culprit was never found; most likely he was a junkie in dire need for cash and a hit. Jake was only twelve years old. His mother suffered severe depression as a result, and ended up sectioned in Garlands Hospital. Heartbroken, Jake was brought up by his regimented grandmother. God rest her soul.

He drove carefully down the thoroughfare, even though the streets were particularly quiet this early January morning. He never took advantage of his status; he abided to all the rules.

Jake was a perfect example of a perfect citizen.

Surrounded by a concrete and corrugated jungle, he focused on the large elongated sixties flat-roofed building, that was surfacing into view. This was where he worked. Tamerton Police Headquarters.

Flurries of light snow landed randomly against the windshield, creating a dancing display of saturating crystals. He turned on the wipers and the heater; a roar of warm air blasted into his face. He revelled in the dry heat as it stroked his clean shaven face. A couple of minutes away from his destination, Jake pondered on the day's agenda. He made mental notes of what he should say during his appraisal. He was very keen to create the right impression, prove to them that he was the man for the job.

Jake also reflected on the extraordinary dream he had in the early hours of the night. It was so perplexing. He found it impossible to remember any detail, just a mixture of moving forms jumping up at him. He was anxious, yes, but not deterred. Shunning his thoughts, he turned left down St. Mark's Road.

Driving into the car park, he felt a pinch of optimism as he pulled up next to Detective Reeves' Mazda estate. Donald Reeves was his boss, mentor and his friend.

It couldn't get much better than this, he thought. *My father would be so proud of me.* A smile lingered and a feeling of pride rippled from within him.

As he got out of his old decrepit car - there was no point buying a flashy set of wheels in this neighbourhood it would only be stolen or annihilated - he marched purposefully to the back entrance of the corroding building. Pushing the doors open with both hands, he entered the vacant and hushed lobby.

Sensing a slight apprehension for the first time this morning, Jake found the silence disquieting. Normally a few colleagues would be busying themselves.

They would be going about their daily duties, coming off their night shift, chatting and issuing pleasantries to one another. Maybe many were on an emergency call out, he mused.

Aiming for the locker room, Jake strode towards the door and peered in. A few lockers were open. Some belongings were scattered randomly; books, a jacket and a boot lay isolated on the laminate floor. Still seeing no sign of anyone, he turned around and urgently walked down the hallway to see if he would eventually hear anyone or find a fellow co-worker.

He then heard a sound.

From an area off to the left of the corridor he heard a squelching lapping sound, rather like a dog guzzling some water.

Focusing on the sound, he trotted to the room calling out for his colleague, Mandy. She usually was in early, chatting happily about her nights out, and how she loved her new found freedom. Jake on the other hand, was content to be in Fiona's life. She was a hairdresser by day and a babysitter by night.

Time alone was indeed precious these days, and when they were together, the wait was well worth it. With that thought, Jake smiled, though his fleeting reflection was tainted with trepidation.

Reaching his destination he grabbed for the door handle, but then violently jerked his hand away. He felt a wet, clammy sensation spread into his hand. Looking down, he saw a coppery substance gel round his palm.

Now fretful, he wiped his hand against his trousers and delved into his belt pouch for his ASP. Looking frantically around him, he found no one else on hand, he was completely alone. He slowly and reluctantly pushed down on the moist door handle, feeling a tremendous sense of dread. His mouth began to dry, his heart hammered. He tried to swallow the huge lump that was forming in the back of his throat.

The door now fully open, he witnessed the vision before him. It left him reeling. He could observe, but could not comprehend the images that his mind was absorbing.

The body of his dear friend Mandy was being consumed by Sarah, the desk Receptionist. She sat astride Mandy, her clawing hands rummaging violently through the contents of her abdomen, ripping out the innards and ramming them into her mouth. Sarah's lips were mottled with a drying flaky skin. Her face was colourless, apart from the claret blood stains that was awash on her sallow face.

Lustfully Sarah lapped and licked a flaccid organ. As she ate, she grinded her vulva against Mandy's sexual parts, throwing her head up in ultimate ecstasy. The liver she gorged was dripping in thick glutinous blood, threads of sticky fibres hanging loosely from the stem of the malleable flesh.

Not immediately noticing Jake, Sarah continued to devour and rub into Mandy, her eyes so wide and wild, they protruded crudely.

Stunned, Jake clenched his baton tightly. His heart thrashed viciously.

Sarah slowly looked look up at him; annoyance now shadowing her face. Having had her meal and sexual gratification interrupted, she was enraged.

Getting up from the ruined remains of Mandy's corpse, Sarah clumsily headed towards Jake. A foul and wretched odour emanated from her gore splattered naked body, draped in half eaten entrails. Jake turning on his heel, he ran out of the room and down the hallway to the overnight cells. Here he hoped to find some of his colleagues or maybe a few prisoners, some allies, backup.

Some explanation.

Behind the locked heavy duty doors, he prayed that he would find some help, a companion even.

Looking behind him as he ran, Sarah was near approaching, the stark strip lights accentuating her blood soaked form. As she followed Jake down the corridor, she still held a piece of Mandy's spleen protectively against her naked breast.

Turning left past posters, events display and helpline numbers, Jake could hear faint strangled cries. They seemed to be coming from the very area that he was heading for. Eager to call out, but reluctant to draw attention to himself; Jake remained quiet. Only his pounding heart, each booming pulse echoing louder than the background noise, reminded him that this was no hallucination.

Suddenly, looming from the gent's toilets, a large form staggered into his path. With a slump, Detective Reeves fell heavily to the floor. Most of his skull was missing. The brain had been gnawed away, white tubercles of cartilage protruded out from the base of the spinal stump, starkly sticking out from Donald's bloody suit's collar. The fear etched on the vestiges of his remaining face, was palpable.

Jake, horrified, ran faster not daring to look at his friend or to find out what or who did this gruesome deed. Sickened, he reached the entrance to the overnight cells, petrified at what he might find. Sarah had thankfully shuffled off, heading towards Reeves' carcass. Jake could hear the distant echoes of mastication travelling down the empty hallway as he fled.

With a sense of irony Jake uttered under is breath;

"Moments like these, you need a fucking gun."

His ASP felt particularly inadequate. It shook within Jake's now tenuous grip, suddenly feeling heavy and useless.

Jake felt defenceless, isolated, frightened.

The thought of finding survivors in this horrific place was his priority. Only then could he flee and escape from this horrendous and hideous nightmare.

The keys were clipped into his belt; this was his only hope to find some other person that was not eaten, or, eating human flesh.

Jake warily opened the door to the corridor that gave access to the four overnight cells. Here he was met with such visual carnage; he felt the bile rise from his stomach into his mouth. Spitting out the acrid vomit, Jake looked around the blood splattered passageway. The mesh covering the long stripped lighting was covered in a gooey substance, reminding Jake of mashed oranges and pureed tomatoes.

The light started to buzz and then it flickered, giving off a murky glow of scarlet light. With Jake looking up, blood dripped onto his nose and into his mouth. A canvas of globulous thick matter, adorned the once white washed wall. The floor was carpeted in gristle, bone, innards and faeces.

Each door was made from heavy iron, containing a food flap and an eye hole. He noisily stumbled against a chair that was lying on its side behind the door from where he came. It was draped in oily viscous blood.

No-one was present at this moment, though he could hear a sound coming from behind one of the substantial doors. The sound was muffled, and it reminded him of someone trying to talk with a gag around his mouth.

Nonsensical burbling was all he could detect. There seemed to be more than one obscure voice, different tones and pitch suggested this. A sound of sloshing water interspersed each muted voice. Jake felt hopeful, maybe some of the prisoners were still alive and with the keys, he could set them free, they could help him escape from this butchery.

As he reached for his keys to unlock the cell, he discovered it was already open. He didn't even have to place the key into the lock; the outside bolt had been released. The door opened easily.

Tina, but with some uncertainty due to the demolished body, and Frank, lay entwined in a bloody and mangled pile. These were Jake's colleagues;

Frank was the civilian night duty watchman, Tina a fellow constable. Each body had been ravaged, torn, mutilated; only their faces remained in one piece.

Surrounding the shattered bodies, human debris littered the floor. Seeing their expressions and how they must have felt as they were torn apart left Jake filled with such repugnance, he crumbled to the floor and wept. He knew that he may well be the next victim to be ravaged.

With a fleeting melancholy reflection, he pictured his parents when they were all together in happier times and also his girlfriend Fiona, going about her innocent daily routine. God, how he wished he could be consumed within her mundane innocent bliss at this moment. Jake longed to see the sunshine, make love and drink a cold beer. In reality he was surrounded by complete devastation and human destruction.

With this notion, he resolutely rose from the floor. He pushed aside splintered bone and flesh with his foot. Wanting an end to this horror and with an urgent hunger to experience normality again, he walked to the second cell. He harboured a fleeting hope that he was not alone in this torturous abhorrence.

The door was unlocked, but closed. He looked into the peep hole. Here, one of his colleagues was feeding upon a torso. The decapitated head lay next to the feeding creature. The face on the head was expressionless this time, but still completely undamaged. The ribcage, spread-eagled apart, lay in a mass of solidifying blood and pulp. The creature that had once been Brian mumbled and chatted to himself as he smeared the thick oozing bowel across his mouth. He then sucked out the stagnant excrement from the entrails. The garbled mutterings that came from Brian was keeping him thankfully distracted; he never noticed Jake's presence.

Carefully Jake put the key into the lock and turned it. He felt a tinge of resolve as he locked the creature in the blood coated cell. Only then did Brian look up, hearing the key as it turned. With his eyes full of malevolent reckless hatred, he leapt up and banged against the door in a violent fury.

Jake, full of disgust, moved onto the other cell door. He felt a strange and sudden sense of detached curiosity and felt more than prepared for the next horrific image that he may face.

The inarticulate sounds became more apparent but still indiscernible as he slowly approached the third cell door. It was slightly open, enabling Jake to scrutinize the inhabitants through the crack in the door hinges.

Three police officers were feeding upon one of the prisoners. Guy, head of Transport Police for the area, had the prisoner's genitals in his fist. The limp and pathetic piece of superfluous skin proved to be of great interest to Guy, as he stretched and tugged at the expandable membrane and then greedily shoved it into his bloodied mouth. The victim was a heavy man, obvious due to the amount of yellowing fat and blubber that lay beside the open and split body.

Jake watched as a horrific possibility occurred. The prisoner may still be alive. Then he did indeed notice the eyes twitching and his legs quivering rhythmically. Jake prayed that the movements were only due to involuntary reflexes.

Trevor, a promising detective constable, was licking the ground. He stuffed urine and blood drenched pieces of muscle and lumps of meaty skin into his slavering maw.

An odorous and vile reek filtered into Jake's nostrils, causing him to gag repeatedly. The other frenzied feeding colleague, that Jake recognised as Stanley the caretaker, had his head inside the prisoner's rib cage. Jake heard the bones splinter apart as the creature burrowed deeper, in great earnest. Again the victim's face was never touched, only a horrifying expression remained.

On the bloody floor next to the prisoners' exposed corpse lay an Alsatian dog; the legs and jaw were snapped and dislocated, as if they were stapled back together crudely and haphazardly. Hanging from the cells barred window, a belt had been twisted around an exposed spinal column, so only the legs hung freely amongst the massacre. No upper body was evident; it probably had already been consumed, stripped clean. The legs were slender, still with stockings, a tattoo on the ankle was that of a rose. Jake knew this to be Linda.

Daily she served him coffee and egg sandwiches at the canteen. Appalled, and feeling as if he was watching the whole scenario from a different dimension. He still insisted to himself that his only chance of survival was to close the cell door without any of the creatures that were once his friends, from noticing.

Standing directly behind the door, he intended to seal the room in the hope that they would eventually consume each other. This indeed was a risky task. Standing away from the spy hole, he took a few deep breaths to prepare himself. When the latch clicked, he would promptly turn the key and bolt the door.

As he began to carefully close the door, an arm immediately thrust through the opening and searched for Jake's throat. The half human shrieked urgently. Jake with all his strength slammed the door shut onto the bony arm, feeling it mash under the weight of the huge door. Forcing the key into the keyhole, with a shaking hand, he turned the lock. The arm hung loosely, twitching spasmodically.

A pained roar came from behind the door. Panting and exhausted, but also relived albeit temporarily, he leaned back and tried to close his eyes. The unrelenting sting of sweat prevented any dark respite from the recent horror. Perspiration and tears then dribbled into his mouth, he could now taste his own fear.

After the previous cells, he was fearful to check the final one, but with his training and his instinctive conscientiousness, he forced himself to walk to the final door. There was no sound coming from this particular cell; just maybe, here he would find a survivor, an ally.

The bolt was unlocked, but the hefty door was shut. He leaned into the eye hole. With a rush of sudden excitement and relief, he saw a man sitting on the edge of the meagre bed. Not an iota of blood or bodily matter cluttered the cell. It was clean and neat. As soon as he felt the elation of finding a fellow survivor that had not been harmed, he suddenly felt suspicious. This was due to the way the man was sitting calmly, reading a book. He was extremely well dressed, his black shoes shone with immaculate brilliance, as did the dark blue suit that was tailored perfectly, although rather dated in its style.

The face was handsome, angular. Ambiguity surrounded his age. Golden hair flopped over his brow as he read his book intently.

Not knowing what to do and feeling a sensation of fresh unease, Jake gingerly opened the bulky door.

The figure now alerted by the opening door, looked up at Jake.

"Can I help you?" The man inquired cheerfully.

Taken aback, Jake felt chilled to the bone; this was not what he was expecting to hear.

"You can't stay here, we have a critical situation!" Jake answered abruptly.

"Yes, I am fully aware of that, and its going well isn't it." The stranger replied arrogantly.

"On your feet, let's make a move!" Jake ordered. Though there was a slight tremble in his voice, he tried to sound authoritative.

"Presently. At least let me finish the page." The gentleman continued to read his book, adjusting his monocle that was carefully placed within his left eye.

Jake realised that the atmosphere in this cell was calm and serene; the walls seemed to emanate a physical glow, their pristine white surfaces reflecting all available light bathing the sole occupant in an enveloping aura of brilliant illumination.

Amazed, Jake moved closer to the man, who at this time seemed engrossed in his book.

Although perplexed by this peculiar man, Jake's hairs on the back of his neck bristled with agitation.

He obviously has no idea what's going on, Jake thought to himself wryly.

"I am ordering you to come with me and to leave the premises, NOW!" Jake started to feel annoyance surface within him, but it was also fuelled with incredulity.

"Jake, you can't tell me what to do!" the man uttered smoothly.

Astounded Jake trembled; he felt he was diminishing into a chasm of unreality once more.

"Who the *fuck are* you?"

With an air of contempt and dismissivness the man simply, yet carefully said; "I am trying to release you from this depravity within which you so gaily dwell. Well, it's been a long time coming hasn't it. Besides I loved this place in the late 1800's. Things were done properly then. High standards, respect, and appropriate punishments were carried out." He added wistfully.

The stranger got up and casually leant forward onto his elaborate cane. He adjusted his cravat and took off his monocle. With a sharper tone and with a chip of intimidation, he continued, "Faces and expressions are like trophies for me, believe me. I do remember them all, and I do mean *ALL*, the good and bad, including yours. Goodbye, Jake."

Jake heard footsteps rapidly behind him, turning around to see who or what was approaching; he clutched his weapon in earnest. Bob Hilton a Detective Sergeant on the force leered towards him, arms outstretched and with a sudden jolt, grabbed Jake and began to tear at his face. Fighting back with immense force, Jake pressed Bob to the ground and pounded him with his ASP.

But the blood coated sub-human was far too strong for Jake.

"Why and how did you do this, who the hell are you?" Jake spluttered in a desperate effort to deliver a coherent sentence.

"Call me a corrector, of a kind. I have come to rid this pathetic society from its low and worthless existence and I have to start somewhere. I know you are one that has tried to lead a respectable and clean life, but quite honestly I have to be brutal. Set an example. No room for sentiment. See yourself as a sacrifice, Jake. It's unfortunate that you, of all people have to see this, but necessary, it is. In the long run, your world will be a better place. I have brought eternal damnation on earth to demonstrate to you and others how you all have become. All I do is touch one person, and they turn into the mirror of today's society." The stranger cleared this throat as Jake continued to battle with the assailant. He then continued.

"So simple, isn't it? You all are nothing more than consuming greedy leeches. You all lust in your own world of profanity and violence. Simply, you have become materialistic, blood draining, selfish, and sexually wanton heathens.

Society today. Good gracious, now we see the true colours. Here, I illustrate to you how society has become. One is getting a taste of one's own medicine dear boy. "

The stranger was staring directly at Jake, holding his gaze as Jake struggled with the creature, the odd compulsion to read his book was now on hold.

Jake urgently fought back. Feeling Bob's huge hand suddenly plunge into his abdomen, his supple flesh tore like fabric. His sternum shattered as Bob rummaged and reached deeply to clutch his beating and frantic heart. Intense pain washed over him, images of random events from his early years up until his present day invaded his mind in flashing sequences. However he still felt the heat of his own blood as it splattered and layered his face. Jake felt the moment his heart was extracted from within him. An odd disconnection. He felt his essence and core amputate. Supreme agony then completely engulfed him, causing him to blackout into an appreciative nothingness.

The stranger sat down as he watched Jake's demise through hooded eyelids, and then continued to read. He licked his fore finger and turned over another page.

SHADOW MAN

Flustered and agitated, Emma stuffed the arm of her young son into the sleeve of his thick padded coat. The threads of a headache were worming around within her head, accompanied with a sense of creeping malaise. After surveying the darkened skies from her kitchen window, she knew rain would be upon them soon.

This was Alfie's fourth day at Nursery. In spite of her weary state, she was revelling in the notion that she would be able to spend a few hours of unadulterated bliss alone. Shopping, visiting the library and being able to sit down for a cup of tea or two was on her agenda, for the first time in many months.

This would be also a perfect time for Emma to reflect and savour the precious snatches of freedom that rarely came her way.

She loved Alfie dearly, but as a single mother, times were hard. Alfie was a needy child, constantly draining Emma with his continued demands. But without him, Emma would have no one, so she rarely complained.

Her only living relation was her mother. She lived up in the crags of the Scottish Highlands, so Emma lived alone along the south coast of England, with only Alfie and the sea as her solace.

Emma bundled Alfie into the buggy, and walked briskly to the Nursery that was only a ten minute stroll. She hummed sweetly to her son who was now showing strains of irritability due to his restless night. He had kept Emma awake with his recurring whining about how he was scared that he wouldn't see his mum again.

"Mum, you will come back won't you?" he snivelled in the early hours of the morning. Emma had reassured him with loving caresses and with consoling words. Alfie finally fell asleep, leaving Emma with a palpitating throb in her head that lasted throughout the rest of the night.

Emma put it down to anxiety due to the new start of his Nursery Education. The two of them were exceptionally close. Having no family around her, and only a few select friends, Alfie and Emma faced the world together, in their own precious and untainted universe.

Reaching her destination, the flurry of mums dropping off their kids reassured her that Alfie was in good hands, and he would feed upon the excitement from the other children.

She kissed Alfie lightly on the lips and ruffled his snowy hair. She then turned and left her little man, who ran straight to the sand area. Smiling in relief, she made her way down the looming hall towards the Nursery's exit. She had a song in her heart and a bounce in her step in spite of the dull ache in her head.

No tears this time.

As she neared the door, she saw a tall man walking with a slight gait coming towards her. Something unsettled her as he neared. She had not recognised him before at the start of the week, but that was not the cause of her unease. A shadow passed her eyes briefly obscuring her vision, but once she refocused; she was alarmed with the way the intimidating man held her stare. A speck of sunlight from the hallway's dusty window caught the nasty scar that ran down the left side of his eye. She noticed as he came closer, a black extended fingernail on his little finger that starkly clashed with the stained grey duffle coat that he wore. Having his hood up, also added to the disturbing appearance. A child followed behind him, so she felt only slightly reassured that he was a father dropping off his child. The child that followed looked up at Emma with cold ashen eyes, she felt a chill pass her soul, a feeling of foreboding consumed her for a second, and then it evaporated once she saw her approaching friend.

"So, I will drop Alfie off at two then, that OK with you?" Shelly voiced with a tinge of stress in her tone. However she had a breezy disposition as she held the hand of her toddler that desperately tried to pull her into the awaiting hall.

"Thanks so much, Shel," Emma responded.

"You are a saint. For you to have Alfie for lunch is a blessing, it means I can go into town, do a few things and have some time to myself." She laughed awkwardly, but Shelly knew the circumstances of Emma's lonely existence.

"No worries, Darlin', you can have your time that you deserve. Mine will be next week. Got my sister coming down so Tim will have a playmate, and that will take some of the load off me!" Shelly laughed rather too loudly and gave Emma a cheeky smile and then chased Tim down the long hallway.

"See you at two!" She called back over her shoulder, her voice diminishing as she and her youngster disappeared down the corridor.

***

After a brisk walk to the bus stop, Emma stood calmly waiting for the number 84. It came into view as she looked at her watch.

I can have a couple of hours in town, she mused as she searched for her purse. The threatening rain eventfully started to patter on the back of her Macintosh, bouncing off the material like plastic pellets. Finally after a final fumble, she found her money and boarded the bus. The smell of ash and fumes filled her nostrils with the stale taste of neglect. She handed the correct fare to the uniformed driver. As she did so, an icy awareness swept over her, along with the déjà vu sensation that rippled her from within.

The driver studied her with an air of knowing. He looked at Emma with a sneer, yet a twinkle in his eye, leaving Emma feeling suddenly unsteady. She felt the grip of disorientation engulf her as she noticed the scar across his eye, and the black fingernail that gripped the steering wheel of the large double-decker bus. Hurriedly, Emma walked into the middle of the bus, sat down and attempted to scrutinise the driver further. Though the bus was busy, she did manage to see his face in the rear view mirror. He returned her gaze with an analytical eye. Emma felt unnerved; she trembled as she fiddled with her bus ticket nervously. Her pulse quickened, her face reddened. Beads of moisture formed on her hairline and the palm of her hands, as the headache hammered within her skull like the constant drumming from a slave's galley.

It can't be HIM. He was walking in, as I was walking out!

These thoughts plagued Emma as she continued to examine the driver. She eventually looked out of the window and noticed her stop was next. The rain continued to splatter, leaving blotches of water on the window, reminding her of bullets shattering on glass.

She walked towards the opening automatic doors as they swished and hissed nosily; the driver was not looking at her as she jumped off the bus into the now heavy descending rain. The bus, with its blackened diesel fumes and droning engine, drove off into the distance.

Trying hard to fathom out how and why a man whose features were so evident and so explicit appeared to her on two separate occasions in the course of fifteen minutes, bothered Emma immensely.

Twins?

No, that's ridiculous!

Still, that was the only conclusion she could come up with as she eventually reached the library soaked to the skin. Wet strands of auburn hair plastered against her face like long sucking leeches.

In her youth the library was her comfort zone, her haven. Here she could submerge herself in books, biographies and history. Feeding upon all the words she yearned to learn and digest. Most importantly she was able to do this in peace. Fingering the books in a carefree manner, she searched for the biography of Grace Kelly. She admired this fairytale film star, who had a fairytale lifestyle and also the inevitable tragic 'not so fairytale' ending.

Such a beauty, such a waste.

Princess Diana had a similar ending, she reflected as she eventually found the book she was searching for.

As she was about to pull the book away from its shelf, she heard a noise coming from behind the bookcase.

A slow shuffling sound.

The library was relatively quiet at this time of day, hence her desire to be here first thing in the morning. With interest prickling her, she made her way towards the area of sound, but was only faced with a hovering shadow that suddenly fleeted past her. Bemused, she looked around, but nothing was visible.

All the aisles were empty, devoid of any presence, but still a faint lumbering sound could still be heard. Banishing any more thoughts of unease, Emma went back to the book she was searching for, pulled it out and walked purposely for it to be scanned.

As she approached the checking out area, she stopped in her tracks.

The man with the scar and black fingernail was there waiting to receive her and her book. He wore a cream thick knitted Arran jumper. His smile was malicious, his eyes cunning. His stare never wavered from hers. His jet black hair was smoothed so brutally onto his scalp; it appeared he had no hair at all. His head reminded Emma of a bowling ball. His skin was pallid, colourless; verging on translucent. He fondled his black nail gently, stroking the vile talon tenderly. He then put it to his lips and licked the inky cuticle, lapping his tongue around the sharp hideous tip. His white and jagged scar ran down from his bushy eyebrow to the top of his snarling bloodless lip.

Emma's heart hammered, an unnatural feeling of trepidation overflowed her being. Panic clutched at her chest, spasms of pain with such heat immersed her head that she nearly keeled over. Dropping the book, she ran outside. She welcomed the cold wet rain that saturated her flushed face and cooled her frantic heart.

Emma had to face the fact that she shouldn't give in to anxiety. Having to face the agonising peril of high blood pressure, Emma felt extremely vulnerable. She religiously took her daily medication and the doctors had reassured her that she was fighting fit, providing she underwent the six monthly checkups and took the daily oral medication. However the uncertainty of a stroke hovered over her like a colossal vulture, ready to consume the entirety of her life, as it did her father. The fear was a constant tragic reminder how precarious life was and how she must value each second she shared with Alfie.

In order to calm her nerves, she turned to the nearest café, sat down, and ordered a strong cup of tea. She sat pensively at her table. Had she known anymore that wanted to frighten her? Did someone hold a grudge against her?

Emma recalled the day, months ago, when she had a mild altercation with a lady in her street and how the husband leered and grinned at her from behind the grimy net curtain.

She reflected on the time when her ex-boyfriend began to get madly possessive with her. But as soon as she fell pregnant he had the temerity to deny that the baby was even his and his interest miraculously disappeared, as did he. However, he messaged her a few times, wanting to start anew, but she knew he would be a lousy father, and an even lousier husband.

She never backed down.

"It could be him trying to get back at me. He knows I get stressed and spooked easily..." Emma whispered to herself as she bit her bottom lip nervously.

Reaching for her bag, she pulled out some tablets for the gnawing headache. She popped out two painkillers from their plastic seal and swigged them down with the cooling tea.

"Everything alright?" The tall blonde waiter hovered over Emma protectively interrupting her thoughts. He had an angelic face, pure and captivating. He was obviously concerned due to her restless state.

"Yes, fine, just a little shaky. Awful headache, but I will be alright thank you."

"Anything I can get you?" His smile was wide, sensual. Emma felt the stirrings of desire trickle within her.

"No, it's ok. I am fine, honestly. Nothing a strong brandy couldn't fix, but hey, it's still early so I will just have to finish my tea and painkillers instead." Emma was feeble at flirting, but she gave it her best shot under the circumstances.

The handsome waiter simply smiled and said,

"I hope to see you here again sometime and maybe I could buy you a drink?"

He took her cup away as she blushed shyly and nodded in agreement. She felt elated and warmed as he turned to leave.

Emma now comforted by the attention from the waiter; her mood lightened as she looked back and studied the slender physique of the gorgeous golden man. He smiled at her as he looked over his shoulder and continued to walk into the mass of tables that cluttered the bustling café.

Her thoughts of the sinister man were now only on the cusp of her mind, not consuming as it was before. Only a sudden shadow crossed her path as she left the café, Emma put it down to a passing car, as sunlight was at last splitting from the skies.

***

The bus journey home was uneventful. The rain had eased, and a sliver of light was trying its best to cut through the membrane of the darkened clouds. The driver was a woman; she had a merry face with a ruddy complexion that reminded Emma of a stereotypical farmer's wife. With her headache finally subsiding, she pondered on the chores that needed doing when she got home as she rested against the smeary murky window. Alfie was not back until two, so she would at least have a couple of hours to read, or watch a bit of TV.

PARADISE.

Jabbing and twisting the key into the lock, Emma walked into her dark hall; thin strips of sunlight from the front door could not penetrate the dinginess of the gloom. Once into the kitchen, checking the kettle was full, Emma slammed the switch down hard. Sitting at the small oval table waiting for the kettle to boil, she started to flick through the pages of her book, kicking off her boots in the process.

A knock at the door interrupted her reading. Feeling annoyed Emma rooted herself to her seat in protest.

"Go away, I want this time alone!" she uttered under her breath irritably.

Thinking that the person had gone, she let out a relieved sigh.

The second knock was more urgent, louder, and lasted somewhat longer.

Grumpily Emma got up from the table, it occurred to her there was a slim possibility it could be her friend Shelly arriving early. It wasn't the postman;

she knew that, he had already delivered the hefty bills that Emma tried so hard to keep on top of.

Another insistent knock pummelled the door. She went through to the front room and peered out from her curtain to see who the persistent knocker was.

From her concealed view, she made out a man in uniform, holding a clip board. Tufts of black wiry hair hung loosely around the collar, but she could not see his face. Looking to her left towards the path, she saw a gas board van that was stationary outside her house.

Oh No, not the bloody Gas Man.

She had to open the door to him, or she would be paying the estimated bill charges, that were double the price if there is no gas reading recorded.

Smoothing the curtain back into place, Emma was about to open the door, when the knocking returned with a vengeance. The booming thud was so loud, it alarmed her. It continued to pound as her heart fluttered and flipped like a bird trapped within a cage.

She jumped back. A sense of disorientation shrouded her as a dizzy spell overwhelmed her suddenly. The headache now so potent brewed within her temples, seeping into the rest of her skull. Nausea swelled from inside her, rising and falling like a surging angry sea. Taking a few deep breaths, Emma leant into the wall to try and compose herself. After the knocking stopped, feeling steadier, she hesitantly opened the door.

Narrowing her eyes in pain and panic, Emma's mind focused solely on the dense and deep pain that pulsed in her head. She let the man in, leaving the door open ajar. Ushering him inside rapidly, Emma pointed to the stairs and spoke in wavering whispering tones as she clutched her head, "Go, there, under the stairs, you will find what you want."

Incensed with the pain she eventually turned to the man, who in returned said; "Miss Williams is it? 27 Grove Avenue?"

Emma in her debilitating pain nodded impatiently due to the obvious question the man asked.

Only then did she notice the black fingernail jutting out like poisonous vipers tongue from the spindly little finger that clutched the clip board.

Eventually in spite of the gruelling pain in her head, she locked eyes with the ominous man as he stood opposite her. Shock so severe, entrenched her to the spot. His eyes began to bugle with enthusiasm as he finally spoke to her in a sickly slithery voice.

"So, you have let me in. That's good. Now you may well be aware why I am here."

Emma's insides tumbled around like a spin dryer as she stood stunned, wracked in excruciating pain as she watched him move closer to her.

The stranger dropped the clipboard. His arms seemed unnaturally long and spindly as he stretched them towards Emma, pointing at her with his long black finger. The visitor forced Emma against the wall, causing the mirror that hung in the hallway to smash to the ground. Shards of glass scattered to the floor like falling icy stalactites as she felt the splinters cut into her feet, feeling tiny particles of glass slice in between her toes. The outsider forcefully clutched Emma's head at both sides squeezing the already inflamed and agonised cranium with extreme vigour.

Unable to scream, Emma could now only see the stranger's eyes that glared with a hint of lunacy as he penetrated and invaded her vision with his manic eyes and sallow leathery skin. Blood veined and murky, his eyes pierced her with a look of such malice, that Emma eventually threw up spilling the contents of her guts onto the lapels of the uniformed attacker, splattering his mouth with chunks of vomit. He licked his lips in pleasure.

"Don't mind me Emma, this happens a lot." The aggressor sneered, as he carefully slid his blackened fingernail into Emma's cornea, penetrating deep within her eye, finally severing the optic nerve. Her eye split and popped like an olive. Blood oozed from the wound, her eye eventually collapsing within the socket. The pain was so immense now that Emma's legs and body shook. She convulsed in pain, throwing her into a chasm of blinding bright heat, her head and body burning from the inside out.

Managing the meagre of whimpers, Emma could only muster a few words;

"Who are you? Why?"

"Why, you know me, Emma, have you not noticed me? Your time is up Emma. It comes to us all eventually, my sweet!" he hissed as he licked his nail clean, like a cat cleaning its paw.

The nail was stained and tangled with parts of cillary muscle and fibrous eye matter. Emma's head hung weakly as he continued to hold her up against the wall with his right arm; his strength unwavering as her body shuddered and drooped loosely. Blood surged from her wounded and annihilated eyeball. The assailant again gouged out the rest of the eye and its contents, clearing all the tissue and membrane until the socket was clean, using his nail like a dental pick.

Panting, and in complete torment, from the corner of her right eye Emma saw the front door push fully open. Standing in the doorway was Shelly and Alfie.

Reaching into the crevices of her dwindling conscious mind, she found the strength to utter a few final words as the stranger let go, her body slumping to the ground like a rag doll.

"HELP ME SHELLY, GET THIS MAN OFF ME. DON'T LET ALFIE SEE THIS!"

Shelly in deep shock ushered Alfie aside and directed him to stand outside the door. She rushed in and held Emma's pulsing head, that was quaking against the hard laminated floor.

"Sweetheart, I will call an ambulance, hang in there, you will be fine."

"*Keep that man away from Alfie!*" Emma spluttered the words desperately as blood curdled in her throat.

"Honey, there is no man. There is no-one here; you are having a seizure of some kind. You are going to be just fine, hold still."

Shelly clutched her mobile in her right hand and called the emergency services, Alfie stood at Emma's feet, weeping weakly wringing his hands.

"Mum...?"

***

Looking on, the evil caller inspected the scene. Only Emma was still aware of his presence.

"Your friend can't see me my sweet. Only you can see me and feel what I do to you. I am your *FEAR*. This is what I look like. I am the one that comes for you before you die. I am the shadow that you see, the perpetual warning that your time is up. Go on, you have one last look at your son and say goodbye."

Emma turned her head shakily, her neck twisting rigidly in the desperate endeavour to see her last vision of her son. Alfie stood alone with such a pained expression of complete sadness and dismay; it consumed Emma with a feeling of utter helplessness. Emma only managed a pathetic lament in the vain attempt for Alfie to know she would be OK. But she knew she was about to die.

"Shhhh, it's going to be fine, shhhh..." Shelly soothed as she continued to cradle Emma's head, nervously waiting for the ambulance.

The Shadow Man knelt down beside Emma's heaving body and with one final deed, plunged his dark claw deep into Emma's ear canal. In spite of the indescribable pain, she could hear the grinding and scraping of the long spiky nail burrowing into her ear drum. It tore into her middle ear cavity and pierced right through to the Cochlea, resulting in her final pain. Her final breath and the final unbearable ordeal of suffering from the stroke that had threatened her all her life was now upon her.

Emma was dying.

Her life subsiding, her world ending, she drifted off into an unknown place. A new fear now faced her. She was so afraid of life and now afraid of death.

Is there no ending to this infinite fear?

This was Emma's last thought as she watched the form of her son, fizzle rapidly away like a burning photograph.

PARANOIA

The window rattled and strummed with the harsh rain as Faye tried desperately to sleep. Sitting up, she plumped her pillows in an effort to feel the comforts of slumber. With a duet of wind and rain pounding on the window, the stormy resonance filled the room with a crescendo of peaking agitation. Faye finally got out of the bed and looked outside.

She glared out of the rain splattered window, narrowing her eyes to focus. Only darkness greeted her as she strained to see if the ferocious gale had caused any damage. Once her eyes had adjusted to the obscurity, she saw that the lime tree was still erect, and her neighbour's roof was thankfully still intact.

Content, Faye turned to go back to bed. But as she did so, a flash of movement caught her eye. A flicker of colour had darted swiftly towards her house from behind the lime tree and she suddenly felt fearful. A sense of dread leaked from her mind, a painful recollection filled her reluctant memory.

Six months ago she had found the strength to leave her violent lover, Ian. In the beginning he had been sweet and considerate to both her and Will, her five year old son. Eventually, a bottle of vodka became his regular evening habit.

He became aggressive, insensitive and accusing.

Many a time he had mocked Will.

"Your Daddy is gone, presumed dead. *Lost in battle*, tough shit. Iraq has got him now. He ain't gonna save ya boy. So what you gonna do about it? Want *ME* to be your dad? *NO WAY*, you little bastard."

Usually, after the mental abuse, the violent punches would start and Faye would take the beatings for her son. Finally finding strength after all Ian's *please forgive me* patter, she and Will moved to a refuge, where they soon built a new and happier life.

She had heard nothing from Ian since. Thank God.

But tonight, the memories haunted her like an insidious shadow that surrounded her being. Abruptly, and with an inner feeling of certainty, she heard the sound of smashing glass. *Was that the back door?*

A falling tree?

She walked to the middle of the room. Here she intensely listened for the sounds she was expecting.

He was back.

He was back now to claim what he thought was rightfully his. She clenched her fists and crept to her door. Thumping blood circulated a pounding rhythm within her ears as she anticipated the next sound.

And She heard it.

Footsteps up the stairs, soft, quiet, steady.

Grabbing the heavy, box-shaped alarm clock from her bedside table, she held it high above her head. The bedroom door opened. She paused, held her breath and slammed the clock ruthlessly against the form that entered the room. With tremendous force Faye bashed and crushed the skull relentlessly as it fell to the floor with a pitiful thud.

Finally opening her eyes she acknowledged her first love. Her missing husband lay broken and bleeding.

Behind the fallen body a futile voice stammered as he held a glass of milk.

"I let him in. He tried to mend the broken window. The tree hit it. Mummy. You killed my Daddy; he came home…"

PRESENCE

The streetlamp stood like a lonely sentinel in a sea of mist. White wispy tendrils gathered around the rays like a halo providing a haven. A circle of light within the darkness created a boundary from the sinister loneliness and bleakness that Lilly knew all too well. She crossed the pavement in order to be comforted by the remaining light that was fifty yards beyond. It served as a beacon of console. The roads were quiet, far too quiet for this early in the evening. The last car had driven passed about ten minutes earlier. She felt isolated.

Yet she always had. She should be used to it.

She was returning from her auntie's 60th birthday party, and as she sadly had not maintained the driving lessons that she had started, she had to walk the half a mile home to the bungalow that she shared. Molly was away again on one of her assignments, but luckily she had let Lilly stay with her for limited rent, as they had been close friends since high school. Molly was an achiever, Lilly was a survivor.

Crossing the road the mist around the light served as a nimbus of comfort, but her anxiety grew. The mist and haze yonder grew denser. She knew that beyond the streetlight her remaining journey was going to be in darkness.

She reached out for her mobile phone. It was buried within the pocket of her dark military jacket that she had saved up for so long, that once adorned a Top Shop dummy in the high street window. Due to her hard work at St.

Stephen's Prep school, working as a learning assistant, she had the funds to treat herself once in a while.

Shame she didn't prioritise her funds for her driving lessons.

Light rain caressed her face. Strands of hair now plastered against her pale features. She blinked away drips of light rain, as her eyes became moist with the precipitation. She turned to her phone and clicked a digit in order for a faint light to radiate. This was better than nothing she thought. As she did so, she shone the phone just above her head. She searched through the pathetic stream of light as she turned left after the last streetlamp finally disappeared behind her.

She walked towards the darkness. Lilly barely managed to see through the shadows. She tugged her coat closer to her body, feeling the icy chill that filled the air. Suddenly she heard a noise that was difficult to identify. It was a dull padding that resounded around her.

She turned. Her hair now moist became flat above her eyes due to the light rain that was continuing to descend upon her.

Lilly was now sure the sounds were footsteps, but the mist behind her had become so thick with murkiness she could see very little and the dense vapour muffled and distorted all sounds. Lilly subtly put her thumb over the 9 over her phone, just in case. She knew she may well be overreacting, she always had and everyone had teased her for being so paranoid all the time.

But Lilly knew.

That was the problem. She 'felt'. She felt too much. She sensed approaching happiness, pain, horror and joy. She felt she was cursed in a perverse kind of way. But lately she had been using this to her advantage.

She actually could feel how others, usually strangers felt about her. If she felt they liked her, that was a huge bonus and she would happily befriend them. Occasionally though, she would feel the hostility, the annoyance of some people, so she kept well clear. Or she saw behind the fake exteriors of some people and then mould them into liking her. She was able to say the right thing if necessary.

Manipulate them.

As the footsteps behind grew nearer, she started to feel a strange aura. A feeling of alarm washed over her. She had this awareness about two months ago when her Grandmother became rapidly ill. She didn't suffer long. Her death was a kind one, if that is at all possible.

As she absorbed this sensation, her skin started to heat up. The warmth rose up from her chest, flooding her neck and face with a flushed prickly glow. However, the surface of her skin was covered in gooseflesh. This was not due to the chill of the rain, but from the surfacing fear that oozed from within.

She quickened her pace. The faint glow from the mobile phone was now serving no purpose as she persisted to stretch it ahead of her in the desperate hope to pierce the gloom.

The footfalls quickened behind her. As they did so she turned, and a dull form of a human appearance took shape. The silhouette walked methodically towards her.

Coming closer.

With a purpose.

She stopped in her tracks, pure curiosity overwhelmed her, but her instinct was saying move on. As the outline became clearer, she could now see an individual wearing a large parker coat, a hood swallowing any features that may have been visible. The figure was now quickly approaching Lilly. In a panicked desperate voice Lilly called out.

"Hi. Are you following me?"

She stifled a nervous laugh and as she did so, the shape abruptly stopped. So sudden was the halt, Lilly felt even more unnerved. Her body shook briefly, her fingers grabbing her mobile even tighter, her legs feeling solid.

Her senses were swelling with fear. Her gift, her knowledge, felt overpowered with danger. But she had a knowing, an understanding that what was about to happen, was meant to be.

The figure remained stationary. No face detectable. Only a sliver of moon peeked out from the inky sky that until now was obscured totally by the solid cloud.

The fur around the hood served as an accentuated menace as the wind faintly ruffled the fibres, leaving a vast void of impenetrable blackness within the hole as Lilly looked inside reluctantly.

Lilly's breath was held for a considerable amount of time before she took a breath. She stumbled backwards catching her heel on the kerb; she was forced to wildly wave her arms out to regain her balance.

Suddenly Lilly's mobile rang. The ringing had broken the silence like a stark shriek in the night.

Hope sprung from the channels of her mind, yet the figure remained static. Lilly started to run.

She ran fast. She managed a couple of feet. Lilly turned and looked back at the figure. It was still stationary, but it was very hard to tell, as her vision was concealed by the ever increasing vapour.

Heart pulsating and mobile in hand, she shakily answered the phone. Her breathy voice trembled as she carried on running the long deserted road ahead of her. Lilly's paces were fast, urgent. She needed to feel secure and this call could be the saving of her fears.

"Hello?"

Silence returned her enquiry.

"Hello?" She repeated, feeling a renewed sense of trepidation.

She was running more rapidly now. Glancing in her wake she saw the figure diminishing behind her into the fog like a fading nightmare from a rude awakening.

As Lilly pounded down the isolated road, the town behind her became dimmer and she yearned to be back in the safe folds of the street life. She again yelled, with so much urgency she was in a state of near hysteria.

"*HELLO, WHO IS THIS?*"

A voice, faint and almost inaudible replied slowly.

"*Why do you run from me?*"

Lilly felt her insides drop and she suddenly halted. She turned her head tentatively to look behind. The figure was yet again upon her, the vast faceless hood gaping out at her. With one hand in the pocket the other up against its hood, she could see the shape holding something to its ear.

"Who the hell are you?" She screamed.

Eventually after a few heavy breaths and a prolonged silence from the caller, courage now took its turn to surface. With sodden hair and chilled body, adrenalin pumping to a degree of defiance, she faced her pursuer head on.

Sliding from the hood, like a turtle from its shell, a face appeared from within the gloomy opening.

It was a face she knew.

It was a woman's face.

Beautiful. Beguiling. Her lips were full, rich and radiant.

Her skin was so pure it resembled milky marble. Her eyes a penetrating green, held an unnerving stare. One chestnut lock of hair hung suggestively over an eye.

Lilly felt that her legs had melted into the pavement like setting cement.

She stared into the face of the caller.

Gazing into the eyes that delved into her soul with a will so strong Lilly felt hypnotised. Immersed.

It was her own eyes staring back from the hood.

Her own features scrutinising hers.

The face harboured such a sallow, opaque exterior that it seemed almost transparent.

For many months now, Lilly was escaping. Running. Fleeing from her own visions and her nightmares.

Now, an understanding descended upon Lilly. She stopped fighting. As she stepped back slowly into the road, the car crashed into her. The sounds of the screeching brakes were the last thing she heard, the headlights were the last thing she ever saw.

Her body flew up into the air like a plastic bag.

As it did so, so did her spirit. Her essence ascended and merged with the mist. Her empty body then fell to the ground with a dull wet thud. As the wheels caught her thighs and crushed her feet; boots and bones turned into mulch.

She watched also as the figure, her angel of death, dispersed into the atmosphere like steam being released from an open window.

Lilly's time was up. She had foreseen her death many a time and in many different ways, which she chose to ignore. Her gift was certainly the blight in her life.

You can never escape your final ending. If you run, it will finally find you. Death is ever present.

TOOLS

Bethany entered Dr Dayes' practise, nausea rising in her gut as it twisted with trepidation. She carried an irrational fear of a man peering so intimately down her mouth, smelling her breath, seeing what she last ate and condemning her personal hygiene.

Shyly, she approached the curt receptionist who looked up in an irritated manner due to her disturbance.

"Bethany Glandon, I have an appointment at 3.30pm."

"Take a seat Miss Glandon." The receptionist ushered her to the seat with her cruel eyes.

Dr Dayes said goodbye to his last patient. He had successfully carried out a root canal. Relishing in the knowledge that his tools had pierced and prodded into the gums, plaque and nerves of his patient's mouth, he rubbed his hands. Steve Dayes had a feeling of ecstasy.

He pierced his pick into the veins of his HIV contaminated wrist. Dots of blood surfaced like emerging bubbles, ready to be popped. The next patient to enter his sterile room would leave with a healthy mouth, but with his unhealthy affliction. The power to make people feel safe, cleansed and satisfied, but at the same time harm them with potential fatality, fulfilled him. His sharp dental pick and clear mirror lay immaculately by his side.

"Hello Miss Glandon." he smirked. "Do come in."

THE ROUND WINDOW

Wide eyed and staring up at the bedroom ceiling, swirls of leaden blackness randomly changed shape as they filled her unyielding gaze. Sharp sprouting buds of sweat secreted from under her hairline as Delilah heard the trundling sound once one. Grabbing the sheets with her moist warm hands that stiffened rigidly by her side, she held her breath once more to see if the strange noise was coming towards her door.

Straining her ears, blood pulsed within her heated head; she heard the heavy lugging continue to heave slowly, rhythmically down the corridor.

It was coming closer.

The sluggish sound shuffled towards her bedroom, interspersed with a metallic clink that fell noisily on the floorboards on the landing. As the sound finally stopped outside her bedroom door, so nearly did Delilah's hammering heart. In the stark contrast of the silence that now surrounded her, the sudden sound of the door knob twisting slowly open, filled her with such a cataclysmic fear that her mind hovered on the brink of a blissful breakdown. She did not want to acknowledge what lurked behind the door. She shut her eyes tightly, screwing up her face in a twisted attempt to hide what was trying to enter her room.

The door did finally open, pounding the wall as if pushed with reckless hate. Again, the shambling movement headed toward the bed, the clinking of metal penetrating in between the sounds of dragging fabric. Delilah finally opened her eyes in the desperate hope that behind the fear of this unknown unexplained horror, there was a plausible justification.

The face of a tattered scarecrow loomed down at her. Crudely stitched eyes of thick thread, carelessly shaped as two large crosses, bulged with mites and larvae as he smirked sinisterly with teeth of sharp shards of animal bone. He was unnaturally tall, his lopsided Panama hat almost touching the ceiling.

Irregular tufts of browning straw protruded from the stuffed woven sack, an abundance of hay escaping from the dishevelled hat that sat haphazardly on the oversized head.

The spectre stretched out his flimsy arms, its hands concealed in the restraints of a straitjacket. Long straps of slithering cracked leather with metal buckles, clanked against the side of the bed, as he reached out to touch her face.

***

Finally turning off the stimulating current that occupied the totality of Delilah's mind, the nurse reached to release the two electrical discs that were attached to Delilah's temples. They were held down with sticky adhesive tape.

Turning to the Doctor in charge, she nodded to him in approval that the task was complete and no adverse side effects had taken place. The Intravenous drip in Delilah's arm remained in place, in spite of the few muscular spasms that took place.

Delilah was wheeled back into her room. Here she remained until she gained a level of consciousness. When at last she opened her eyes she was greeted with a heavy headache and aching limbs.

God, she needed a drink. More so now, than she had done in the entirety of her life. After coming to Mark Glaton Rehabilitation unit within the bowels of London, she had never felt so alone and so imprisoned with patients that frankly terrified the life out of her.

Accepting a life of sobriety was until now, something she had never considered until the fateful day she fell in the street and convulsed due to a massive seizure. The shame and embarrassment of losing control publicly and in front of her relatively new boyfriend who had no idea she was a dependent drinker, was the turning point in her life.

The dawn of her realisation.

Suffering years of depression and hiding it behind the poisoned shroud of alcohol, Delilah's life was nothing but a facade. No one suspected her hidden dependency as she worked as a Librarian. This was a job she actually enjoyed and a job she could *hide* behind, as she did with the alcohol. After years of relying on her 'friend' the wine box, Delilah believed also that she was leading a life of normality. The depression had eventually become part of her, rooted within her essence. The wine however was the tool to banish it, mask and shield it from others, and to a degree, from herself.

Now she was going to lead a life of sobriety.

This was her wish, her new testament and she was going to do this for her family, and most importantly for herself and her self respect.

Clumsily, Delilah tried to sit up. Successfully, she managed to reach her calves that were taut and aching after her ECT therapy. Her stomach churned and swirled with large amounts of vomit and bile as her hands shook like juddering robotic limbs. This was her second day without a drink. She was now coming face to face with the effects of withdrawal. The Benzodiazepines and Thiamine they pumped into her every four hours, helped ease the first strains of nausea, shakes, sweats and Delirium Tremens.

Until Now.

"They always said day three would be the worst...." Delilah whispered to herself as tentacles of panic started to squeeze her from within. Looking around her the walls were white washed and bleak, fragments of peeling paint were the only contrast on the blank bare walls. The single window that was curtained with

a green flimsy fragment of fabric adorned the rusty barred window, reminding Delilah of a Victorian gaol. A worn out wooden desk that was chipped and scratched, supported a vase of daffodils that looked out of place in the stark colourless room. A metal folding chair with plastic seat and back stood forlornly waiting for an occupant.

Delilah's door remained closed. A small yellow stained curtained window for the orderlies and nurses to observe the patients, remained open.

Starting to feel the impact of her withdrawal more severely, Delilah groggily got out of the bed, rubbing the sides of her throbbing head. Her trembling body undulated with waves of spontaneity as Delilah headed for the door. She clutched the side of the wall as a guide, but also in the hope that these firm barren structures would prevent her from falling weakly to the vinyl flooring.

Opening the door, she faced a long echoic corridor, again with the same blue vinyl flooring that resonated with shuffling feet and wails of profanity and pain from the other patients. The ECT treatment may have helped with her depression assumingly, but the unrelenting surge of agitation and disorientation came to Delilah with such force that she was desperate for some medication, or realistically, a good strong drink.

Edging her way out down the corridor that was littered either side with replica rooms, Delilah headed towards the medication hatch. Here she would be greeted with the meds she craved, along with the other patients that would line up desperately waiting for their welcomed relief.

She hoped to find some treatment for the pain in her head and for the tremors that were now rippling through her body like convulsing electrodes.

Delilah was scared. She felt out of control. Her whole body shuddered as if shaken by the invisible hands of an angry child irritated with her unresponsive rag doll.

Delilah had sustained her lifestyle through alcohol, and now she was alone and desolate. Her crutch, her side kick and friend now were gone. She felt abandoned and bereft. Like a small infant suddenly bereft of parental attention, she had to face the rest of her life alone, without any guidance from a guardian or mentor.

In spite of the overpowering feeling of crapulence, Delilah noticed a corridor adjacent to her as she crept down the hall. Curiosity fuelling inside, accompanied with the frenzied fever that swelled within her, Delilah nevertheless trudged towards the large round window that beguiled her. Its perfect clarity, pure and inviting amidst the cold plaster walls, intrigued her. *What lay behind this window?*

Still sliding her hands carefully along the cool but crumbling walls, she shuffled her way finally to reach the window. Slow cautious steps, each sending her body into quivering ripples of nausea, caused her body to drip in her own salty sweat. Her dressing gown hung loosely around her thin body, the belt gathering dust from the worn out floor.

She peered into the round window. It was the size of a porthole from a cabin cruiser; no curtains veiled the curricular paned glass. Grabbing her navy blue towelling dressing gown closer to her shivering body, Delilah took a sharp intake of breath as she saw the vision before her.

She was looking into her own bedroom.

The same floral prints adorned the pale blue painted walls, two inbuilt wardrobes spewed out a few of her clothes that randomly fell onto the littered floor.

Her bed was empty, unkempt.

Standing at the end of the bed, the scarecrow hovered looking up enquiringly, its head cocked to one side as if waiting for recognition. Delilah closed her eyes for a second, in the slim hope that she may be hallucinating due to the withdrawal, but when she opened her eyes again, the face of the scarecrow was up close to the window. The twisted grin and bulging straw head that was riddled with bugs and worms, snarled back at her with malicious expectancy. Two large woollen stitched crosses gazed at her blankly. Delilah fell to the floor screaming, burying her head in her arms.

***

The injection pieced her buttock with an angry bite. The vitamin B1 shot along with the Valium and Lithium did manage to soothe Delilah as she was scrutinised by the unit's staff. An orderly and nurse were quick to reach her cries after her fall, carrying her onto a gurney and wheeling her briskly to an examination room.

"You are going to be just fine." The nurse smiled as she put the syringes into the tin plate then turned to wash her hands.

Delilah watched her as she picked up the utensils that she had used and began to sterilise them.

"So, it's normal to hallucinate then? I have never experienced this before, it's terrifying me. I don't know if I can face another shock like that again."

Delilah's voice was calmer now, almost expressionless as the medication started to filter through her veins.

"Don't worry too much, honey. These meds you are on now will ease them. Tonight I will confirm with the Doctor that you can have a stronger sedative so you sleep better and sleep undisturbed."

The nurse was a well rounded comfortable African, whose motherly approach stirred something inside Delilah.

"Here's hoping." Delilah replied, as she carefully slid off the examination couch and smoothed down her wet hair and crumpled nightwear.

Leaving the tiny room, she thanked the kindly nurse that had rescued and sedated her, then started to head back to her room. She wanted to record her experiences here in this unit; keeping all coherent memories recorded in her leather black bound diary.

Walking past the pool table that was in the middle of the hall, she watched a couple of patients playing a game. One was an old man, looking worn and haggard, but he did have a twinkle in his eye, or maybe it was the drugs that kept him so jovial. He found it hard to hold the cue steadily, but gave it his best shot nonetheless. The other man was in his mid twenties; he looked confident and cheeky, but he also was very pleasant to his opponent, jollying him along but nevertheless seemed to delight in the fact that he was ripping strips off his challenger.

"Want a game when you are up to it? Looking at you now, I bet it's going to be a while. Hellish isn't it when it's at this stage." The young man placed his cue on the side of the table, and winked at his opponent indicating that he wouldn't be long. The rugged gent ruffled his fibrous beard and raised his hand in agreement.

Delilah merely nodded, a faint smile tried to spread across her wan and pale face that was now showing signs of swelling with fresh blotches of pink flushes.

"It's easy; pot the balls into the holes! When you are up to it, give us a shout. I am Greg by the way, and if you need a chat, or need some help with this fucking shitty hell you're in, remember I have come through it. I know what it's fucking like – but it does get better, honest. "

Unable to communicate any further, Delilah nodded her thanks, genuinely glad someone showed her some warmth and wandered unsteadily back down the long brightly lit corridor.

***

Back in her room Delilah sat on the bed. At least she was making acquaintances now. Greg seemed to be of a similar age and looked as though he was on the final leg of his treatment here.

Maybe it will be OK, maybe I will recover from this.

Feeling fine threads of hope for the first time; she clambered onto the bed and lay down. She focused on the ceiling above wondering how many other patients had lain on this very bed, experiencing the same thoughts and emotions as she was currently enduring.

Did they manage to beat the demon? Did they go on to lead a clean life? Did they eventually kill themselves due to the sheer upheaval of accepting sobriety?

Abruptly the bed shook from either side. The shuddering surrounded her as she grabbed either side of the single bed urgently. Shaking with fear but also with the force of the juddering activity, Delilah and the bed vibrated with a regular thump. The bed sheets fell to the floor in rhythmic time with the pounding.

With great effort, Delilah managed to sit up and leaned over to see what was causing the shaking. Hair falling towards the floor, Delilah gazed under the bed, holding on with all her strength.

Under the bed, lay the scarecrow. His arms pushed up against the springs within the metal frame, forcing the mattress to shake as he pounded the surface. His makeshift dishevelled legs were apart, holding up the sides of the bed that continued to kick with a brutal force. The buckles of his straitjacket clinked on the ground with each subsequent push. Slowly, yet calculatingly, his head turned to look at her and the shaking stopped as suddenly as it started.

Delilah did not scream this time. She sat up, as the bed became still and static. Though she did not show any display of fear, her heart hammered rampantly within her chest. The silence in her room was blaring. The anticipation of what was going to happen next gripped Delilah.

After an excruciating wait, Delilah reluctantly and hesitantly lowered her head to see if the thing had gone.

He Hadn't.

He was still waiting for her.

Watching her.

Slowly, he slid out from under the bed, straw scraping and scratching as he dragged his floppy body away from dark recess.

Delilah jumped off the bed, and ran to the corner of her room. A scream stuck in her throat as the scarecrow lumbered towards her awkwardly and disjointedly. He came face to face with her and reached for her throat. In desperation Delilah grabbed for his head that was a coarse hessian sack, and ripped it off with such force, that the rough twine that held the rugged bag together split, the head tearing from the malleable shoulders.

Oozing and pouring out from the gap in the neck, a hoard of tiny spiders swarmed out, scurrying wildly onto the rest of the staggering body; that then fell to the floor in a heap of straw and fabric. The scourge of spiders scuttled unexpectedly towards Delilah's feet, crawling up her legs in an angry pursuit. They swarmed up finally into her private parts, dispersing into every crevice of her torso, eventually coating her whole body as if she was wrapped in an animated brown carpet. Her entire body became submerged in the hoard of wriggling arachnids.

Overcome with the fear of choking on these tiny frantic creatures, Delilah remained silent. She could only watch in despair as she saw the flimsy straight jacket gather itself from the floor, forming back into the scarecrow. His long spindly buckled arms reached down for the limp sack that was its head, and clumsily attached it back to its gaping opening. Miraculously, its body and head suddenly gained substance and form, filling out completely with revived straw and sawdust.

THIS IS NOT HAPPENING TO ME YOU ARE NOT REAL!

Delilah finally collapsed to the floor, her last thought echoing in her head as she drowned within a sea of spiders and wretchedness.

***

Delilah came round to a flurry of blurred faces looking down on her. There was no sensation of crawling spiders engulfing her now, only a stark light with hazy images, softly chattering inaudible mutterings.

"Has he gone?" Delilah managed to utter these words feebly as she tired to lick her dry mouth and chapped lips.

"You seem to be having some adverse affects with the medication we gave you for the withdrawal symptoms. So we have now revaluated your medication and dosage. We are giving you something else that hopefully won't react with you in this negative way."

The doctor in charge had a kind smile, but hard and tired eyes.

"We will take you back to your room now, and assess you through the night, so you will not be alone for too long. Are you happy with this, Miss Beck?"

"Thanks, but I am so scared he will come back…" Delilah slurred as she slipped back into the welcoming harmonious sleep as they wheeled her back to her room.

***

It had been three days, two nights and Delilah had no visitations from the terrifying monster that had plagued her since she decided to change her life.

Lining up at the canteen, Delilah felt that things were going to be positive for the first time. Her withdrawal symptoms were now under control, the heavy dosage of diazepam made sure of that. Optimism and motivation gradually bloomed inside her like a young foetus growing in the safe harbour of a mother's womb.

"…Yes, I leave on Friday, my Dad is picking me up at eleven." Delilah answered Greg as he asked her when she was leaving.

"Well I leave tonight Delilah, and I am so petrified of facing the world without the drugs. I managed to cope with them you know? They made me function, not be afraid, but now…" Greg sighed and looked to the ground then continued, "But it's good to be clean and I am gonna make it work this time Delilah, but the fucking *temptation* is always gonna be there, ain't it?"

Sighing once more he looked down at his untouched plate. He picked nervously at his finger nails that were coated in purple nail varnish and then continued again,

"I really am going all guns to lead a normal life, for the first time in my life!"

Delilah rubbed his ornately tattooed arm.

"I know, it's the same for me, but you will do it. You have the right attitude. You want this to work Greg. *I* want this to work for you. *If you believe you can, you can*! You won't give into temptation *if* you don't want to."

Delilah looked deeply into his worried eyes. Their gaze lingered. She then continued, her tone lighter.

"But hey, we must exchange numbers and keep tags on each other. Be each other's conscience in case we slide back down that slippery slope!"

"Deffo pretty lady, we will do just that. I will come and say my goodbyes later on today and give you my number. Thanks for being my bud here, it's good that I came here to get clean, and get to meet a gorgeous babe in the process!" Delilah blushed, a feeling of calm settled inside her.

The time came for their goodbyes. They kissed, hugged and cried; leaving Delilah suddenly feeling that old familiar pang of abandonment creep within her.

Did she want a drink?

She asked herself this question, and fought the turmoil that started to brew from the recesses of her mind.

NO, she didn't. No yet, anyway.

Elated, she felt the stirrings of hope filter through her veins that cleansed and extracted the poison that once soared through her blood. She watched Greg depart, with a feeling of determination and promising resolution. She was experiencing faith for the first time. Hearing Greg talk optimistically reassured this feeling.

She was going to beat this, she was going to be in control of her life, not let the evils of dependency drag her down to the gutter; she had been there for far too long.

***

Back at home, her parents tiptoed around her, trying almost too hard to make things comfortable, too perfect. The actual issue of her addiction was never addressed, still a huge taboo within the family. Her boyfriend had been supportive to a degree, but after he had visited a few times he realised that his embarrassment far outweighed his sense of duty to his girlfriend and the visits soon stopped. But this was the least of Delilah's worries right now.

She was constantly thinking about the scarecrow. *Why had it been so god damn real?* His image had been haunting Delilah for a while now, even after three weeks of tranquil temperance.

She had asked Greg over the phone the other week if he had hallucinated, but he said his nightmares were far worse than he had ever experienced, however he had never actually believed that his dreams could ever be real.

Delilah broke the final egg into the bowl, cursing as a fragment of shell fell into the dark yellow glutinous yoke. Picking up the whisk, Delilah vacantly started to beat the eggs into the deep dish. She was lost in thought as rhythmic beats rattled within her head along with her deliberations.

Why had she started to drink? What caused her to be so dependent on alcohol?

She knew. Deep down.

She didn't need a doctor to tell her.

It was her lack of self esteem and the constant *fear* of people. She felt people judged and mocked, making her feel worthless. It was the *fear of life* itself that she couldn't come to terms with. Having no self belief or self love, she had nothing. She feared society, and she feared failure.

Her feeling of inadequacy overwhelmed her constantly, but with a glass of wine or four, she was believable and credible, she actually believed this herself. Confidence poured out of her, she was in control. Her inconceivable shyness was obliterated. Others felt and saw that too, or so she thought.

Yes, she knew why she depended on alcohol, because she couldn't believe she could depend on herself.

A knock on the patio window startled her as she turned round to see who was at the glass door.

The scarecrow rapped on the glass window snarling, its teeth covered in mashed insect flesh. As Delilah dropped the whisked eggs to the floor, the intruder began to slide open the unlocked door. Stepping into the kitchen as if he had a right to be there, he bumbled his way towards Delilah. His body was vulgarly stuffed with dispersing straw and sawdust, secreting spiders and lice.

He followed Delilah uncontrollably into the front room. The TV was on; 'Good Morning Britain's' banal ramblings filled the room.

Delilah backed herself onto a chair knowing that she had no where to go as the ominous figure approached her with great speed in spite of its clumsy form.

From the dark abyss of her soul, she suddenly felt a bizarre unfamiliar feeling, but it felt natural to her at the same time. Confused but determined, Delilah instinctively knew it was a feeling of retribution. She knew what she had to do.

"GO AWAY FROM ME NOW. I AM NOT AFRIAD OF YOU. I DO NOT NEED YOU ANYMORE. YOU CAN NOT CONTROL ME LIKE YOU DID. I DO NOT NEED YOU!"

The scarecrow retreated, stumbling backwards as if in shock. Delilah, still clutching the whisk got to her feet, and with all the inner strength she could muster, she walked towards the very thing that had terrified her most.

With an air of quiet confidence, Delilah grabbed the shoulders of this physical manifestation and shook it with such aggression that it started to recoil away from her. She shook and punched until her strength was finally sapped from every pore of her body.

Opening her eyes she saw nothing. No scarecrow that was bound in a hideous straitjacket, with stagnant straw entwined with spiders faced her.

All that remained was the tea towel that was clutched in her hand, and the whisk that lay on the carpet like a discarded memento.

***

The anthromorphic personification of her inner demons failed to rear its ugly head again, though there were slivers of memories that pricked her thoughts like sharp shards of broken glass, cutting through and piercing the layers of her conscious mind. Delilah's veracity would not let the terrifying vision affect her life anymore. Having tasted the sweet tranquil knowledge that she could be free from the cruel teasing grip of alcohol, Delilah welcomed her new found strength into her heart that now pumped around freely within her veins like a cleansing river of the purest, crispest mountain water.

Delilah finally found the power and belief that she was a lovely person, and that she had this strength all along. It was only hidden, waiting to be discovered. Confidence dwelled with her core, but it was concealed within her shyness and self loathing. She had every right as anyone to walk and be accepted on this plant.

She cherished her new life; she cursed herself knowing she had wasted so much of her existence in a cloak of denial.

There were certain times nonetheless that niggling gnawing need for a drink surfaced, particularly on social occasions and fleeting moments of loneliness. But the shuffle of straw a clink of a buckle, reminded Delilah that her confidence and renewed sobriety could banish the hideous ogre that manifested itself as her temptation and addiction.

CHECKING OUT

Izmir 1960

Emily clutched her cumbersome belly and waddled into the Turkish hotel room. The muted tones of Elvis Presley's 'It's now or never' drifted up from the room below.

She knew it was time. Pain ravaged her body within ten minute intervals.

Keeping this pregnancy from her husband had been no easy task, insisting her weight gain was simply hormonal with the added fluid brought on by her anti-depressants.

As a respectable lawyer, having a baby at this time would cripple her career. Her job would be surely jeopardised. She was on the cusp of becoming a partner with her current employer.

A rare feat indeed for a woman. Nothing could come between this pivotal opportunity. Having this child would also lead to the loss of her independence and eventually, her husband. Seeing her husband was certified as sterile, he would know immediately that she had been unfaithful. If he found out about the fling with a young waiter he would disown her and the money therefore would be greatly reduced.

Money was her happiness. Money gave her an abundance of freedom. And love? This was not a priority or an emotion for Emily

Saunders. It was merely an act of sentimental rubbish and a false feeling of warmth when one wanted a screw.

Her love was money. She made good money herself, but the extra financial benefits that came with her prestigious husband was far too important to throw away. But there was something she *would* have to throw away, and it looked like today was the day.

In the last month of her uneventful pregnancy she had flown to Turkey, *on business* to escape the scrutinised looks and to escape her questioning spouse.

Emily sat on the bed. Lying next to her was a large book. She flicked to the page that she needed, and she started to read.

Under the bed were four plush ruby towels and newspapers. A suitcase that contained a sheet and a pair of large scissors also were tucked under the valance. Emily had bought them from the local market last week when the first twinges began to appear.

The pain subsiding temporarily, she hoisted herself off the bed and reached under for a towel. As she did so, pain entrenched itself into her belly, her back rigid with fiery onslaught. The contraction was so severe her body went into shock. Her knees buckled and shook, creeping chills engulfing her skin as her teeth started to chatter.

She felt so cold.

Kneeling on all fours she tried to breathe calmly through the unforgiving attack of pain. With her strawberry blonde beehive hairdo sloping unceremoniously to one side, her body quivered fiercely. After two minutes of agony she found some momentary relief and finally got up and returned to the bed. Before the next bust of agony Emily returned her gaze to the opened page of her book.

What happens when you have an emergency birth at home?

Emily skipped the obvious advice but before she could skim to the final paragraph, a blast of pain so intense flooded her body along with the powerful urge to push.

"Shit! It's coming..!" Emily shrieked into the pillow as the terrific pain overwhelmed her. She could feel the baby burrowing down deep inside her, the birth canal and cervix stretching and contracting with each explosion.

"*FUCK!*" Emily had never experienced such pain.

Every two minutes her body contorted, inside and out as she struggled with the torture. In the respite of her suffering, Emily simply cursed, she hated this baby as deeply as the pain it now inflicted upon her. Another gulf of extreme pain ripped inside her as she left the bed and undressed, kicking her knickers into the corner.

Wearing only a blue and white gingham checked shirt, she got to her knees and rocked herself through the unrelenting ache. As the urge to push became inevitable she lumbered back to the bed, grabbing the towels with her. She laid the towels carelessly out and heaved her body onto the firm mattress.

With an audible *pop*, waves of water gushed out of her as she felt the baby's head crowning, its soft downy hair cresting from her engorged vagina. She so wanted to grab the thing out of her in one swift swoop, just to get rid of it from within her pulsating tormented body.

With one almighty push the head emerged, slopping out of her instantaneously. She gasped, feeling an element of relief from the terrific trauma her body and mind has experienced.

Then again the seeping pain surfaced and with another push the baby's body came out, emerging out of her like a lump of wet fish.

Relieved it was almost over, with baby still attached to the multicoloured cord, she reached and searched under the bed.

The baby bleated like a newborn lamb, as she cradled it between her knees.

Emily finally found the suitcase. In her strained and perspiring state she managed to open the case and reach the scissors, the blades shimmering in the hot brilliant sun. As the baby lay helpless between her legs, the wrinkled red body was smothered in white waxy vernix; it started to whimper. She began to cut the cord.

"Easy, there you go. You are out of me now. We are at last *Disconnected.*" Showing nothing but contempt, she wrapped the newborn in a towel. As she looked into her baby's eyes, a sudden and unexpected exchange took place.

A moment of silliness, a false instinct of love that's all. However, a connection was made, but Emily dismissed it as a fleeting feeling of fancy.

She felt nothing for this child at all. As she waited for the placenta to be delivered a huge chasm of pain resurfaced. The same extent of agony ripped from within, along with another urge to push. The placenta was coming, but to her horror another child's head protruded as it descended out of her bleeding inflamed vulva.

This time Emily screamed. Her shrill torturous yell reverberated throughout the room, bouncing off the walls and returned to her own ears.

As the second child fell out of her so did the placenta. Reaching for the bloodied scissors once more she snipped the other cord.

"Twin boys…I don't believe it…" Now weeping she gathered the second baby and wrapped him up. The other baby lay quietly, studying his mother as he lay at the bottom of the bed. Swallowing emotions that she thought she would never experience, she became suspended in a complete feeling of ambivalence.

Did she feel love? They are so adorable! Now you are a mother Emily, you have to look after them. I hate them. They are so…beau…They have cursed me!!!

All these turbulent thoughts travelled within her chaotic mind, as she placed her second son between her crossed legs. Reaching forward to the end of the bed, she stroked the quiet son who watched her expectantly.

"Hush little baby, don't say a word…"

After her macabre lullaby she grabbed the remaining towel and placed it against the tiny head of her firstborn son. She held the flannelled fabric over his head, sobs of remorse yet anger and hate convulsed within her. The other twin suddenly started to squall. He would also meet his death the same way and join his brother in the arms of oblivion.

A door opened.

In broken English the Chambermaid stuttered, "I heard screaming, Miss…?"

Stunned at the scene in front of her, the maid almost swooned. *A mother smothering her baby with a heavy towel as she balanced another one on her crossed knees? This was unconceivable.*

Sweeping the screaming child from Emily's lap, she shrieked at Emily to stop, but it was too late. The infant now lay motionless. Silence filled the room. Both women held their gaze as the surviving baby's desperate lament began to cease.

"What have you done?" whispered the Turkish maid, her black tresses falling around her olive skin. Looking down at the child that was now cradled in her arms, she instinctively protected it. The baby rooted for milk against her clothed but ample breast.

"I have killed my baby…My baby. I hate them. Take the other one away from me before I do the same to him…HELP ME! Oh my sweet baby…"

Emily could only rock to and fro as she welcomed the pleasing side of insanity flood through her. Sitting in blood, water and discarded cord, she hummed a lullaby for her dead baby. Here she would escape to the recesses of her mind where no one could touch her and no memoires would filter her now closed mind. She was locked in a safe place now, no pain and no shame.

She would miss no one, as she had never loved anyone enough to miss, until…

The chambermaid looked on as the woman continued crooning softly.

***

1994

Cahid trundled up the stairs with the small suitcase and holdall. Blonde wisps of hair stuck to his tanned cheeks as he lugged the suitcase into the lobby of 'The Oasis' hotel. In spite of its small size, the suitcase seemed extremely heavy. The woman behind him looked ordinary enough, but the manner in which she darted and gazed at her surroundings fretfully, unnerved him.

With the over use of eyeliner and the exaggerated lip line, she looked like a desperate lady wanting to hold onto her youth. Cahid guessed she must have been in her mid sixties.

After returning from the USA he was happy to be back home.

To the place where he was born.

His Mama who now owed the establishment was in failing health, so coming home to help out with the business was the least he could do.

His advertising company that he co-owned could cope without him for a while and he so desperately wanted to return to his roots. It had been a long time.

Happy memories of intimate family life, long summer days mooching around the bazaars and dipping into turquoise lakes, filled him with joy. Although his paler skin and blonde hair made him different from the rest of his adoptive family, they embraced and accepted him as a brother and a son.

However being a porter was not the most idyllic of jobs. Being a receptionist was even less enthralling. The clientele were usually so stuck up, dismissive and damn right rude.

Bloody foreigners.

Entering the opening door of the lift, they stood in silence. The doors drew to a close with a heavy muffled hydraulic glide as Cahid dumped the suitcase down.

"Lovely weather you are having." The woman broke the awkward silence as the lift slowly ascended up the shaft.

"Yes indeed Madam, it's like this almost all year long. I hope you don't find it too uncomfortable. What room number are you?" Cahid remained polite in spite of the edginess that reflected in his voice. Before the woman could answer, the lift hissed and jerked to a sudden halt.

Looking around herself the woman looked even more uptight. Cahid rammed the lift button repeatedly to the top floor. The stainless steel walls that surrounded the tiny compartment reflected their images, distorting them into disturbing forms.

"Don't worry, sometimes this happens. There is an emergency button." The woman smiled awkwardly, her makeup melting before his eyes as sweat dripped down from under her furrowed brow.

To make conversation Cahid asked about her holiday.

"So what brings you here? Family, friends? A long earned vacation?" The lady was studying him scrupulously.

"I have been in hospital for the last thirty six years. I am returning to lay my demons to rest."

Cahid was surprised with her retort and thought he would change the subject quickly.

But the woman continued nevertheless.

"I had a baby in one of these rooms. He was taken away from me, so now I am looking for him. They told me that the woman who worked here adopted him and now I want to lay things to rest. Thank her."

A violent spasmatic chill poured through Cahid, as a certain realisation struck him.

He had been told that his birth mother was British and had secretly given birth to twin boys within the walls of this hotel. One twin did not survive and due to the trauma of the birth and death of her baby, she had been committed to a secure unit for the insane. He was indeed that surviving twin, and the woman he called Mama who had discovered the tragedy, had mercifully adopted him.

"I am so sorry. So you are now looking for your son *here*? What guarantees do you have that he is still around these parts?" Cahid's voice trembled, so he coughed to hide his embarrassment and astonishment.

"I just know. Call it motherly instinct. I never thought I would feel that pull of longing. But after many years being assessed and time to reflect, I have had a change of heart. I need to meet my son once more and tell him how I feel. I want to see how he has grown. If he is happy…" The woman suddenly stopped, a tear emerging from her light blue eye.

"Well. Here I am Mother. You have found me. I am your son."

The rush of emotion after his sudden outburst almost keeled Cahid over. He wobbled and placed his hands to the side of the lift to regain his balance. His face flushed with awkwardness, hope and fear tingled his skin as thin threads of perspiration dripped down his side burns like slimy lines of oil.

The woman's face for the first time held on evidence of emotion. The atmosphere within the small stifling space suddenly turned cold. Her static stare intimidated him. Gone was the nervous look, the tear.

Replaced was a face of granite. The severe lines that etched her down turned month started to waver, as she finally spoke after the excruciatingly long silence.

"My, this *is* interesting. Who would have thought it? I have been thinking about you for, let's see…" Emily paused as she reached into her ample handbag. She continued slowly. "Well, everyday actually. Every day of my life I have been thinking about you and thinking about what I would do to you once I have found you."

Cahid was confused; shaking, he felt waves of nausea somersaulting within his gut.

"Er, well is that a good thing or a bad thing?" Cahid nerves could not be concealed within the forced laugh.

As Emily continued to rummage inside her bag, the lift finally sparked into life ascending once more with a jolt, the drone breaking yet another suspended silence.

"It's a bad thing, I am afraid. You see, if it was not for you, I wouldn't have had my life taken away from me. My home and job. My husband. At least I managed to rid your brother, what a little miserable wretch he was."

The lift opened; fresh air filled the stuffy cubicle. Cahid was about to run out as Emily found what she was searching for. The claw hammer's ugly talon loomed into Cahid's face, the first blow striking him against his temple. Falling to the floor be grabbed his face. Torrents of pain swamped him as blood gushed from the opening wound.

Emily began moving towards him to strike yet another blow, but suddenly screamed. Her sleeve became stuck within the closing lift, dragging her arm to the ground and forcing her body to follow the flow.

Slumping to the floor and now on eye level with her son, she waved her free hand aggressively that still clutched the hammer. Her intention was to thrust another strike into her son's already bloodied head.

"*You bastard, you ruined me and now I am here to ruin you.*" With one final wave of exertion, she released the hammer and threw it into the side of Cahid's neck; the thud of the hefty weight causing him to curl into a ball and howl liked a kicked dog.

At the commotion a young female guest exited from one of the rooms. Watching the scene in disbelief she screamed for help, running down the fire exit. In the interim, Cahid managed to sit himself up.

"How could you do this to me? I thought you had a change of heart and wanted to find me…" Eyes filling with blood from his violent gash, he watched as his mother spat out her final words.

"*I have no heart. That's why I am here, to clear up unfinished business. But once again, you have stopped me.*"

The massive heart attack was a blessing, but not a deserved one. Emily lay in a crumpled mess, her breaths slow and laboured. Sounds of everyday life filled the corridor, the buzz of market life and stridulating crickets were muffled against the heavy swell of sorrow and pain that filled Cahid's aching heart.

He watched as his mother finally died. She held her gaze with Cahid, her eyes wide with fear yet wide with hatred. Emily's final gasps of life wisped away from her open mouth, dispersing like a morning mist.

"Why? How can you hate so much? We were only babies…we would have made you happy…Surely?" The wail of approaching sirens filled the warm air and then faded, as Cahid slid into unconsciousness.

RETRIBUTION

The dreams had been too vivid and disturbing for Danni. She awoke with a start, her body numb and rigid from the tension that fuelled her fitful night. Strobing images still filling her blurry head, she turned onto her side. After her extensive sweating, the sheets were now moist and chilled.

She gazed at the cold empty place where her cold and empty husband had previously been. These days, he never bothered sleeping with her. If he felt the need for some rough sex, he would creep into the double bed, throw her over onto her front and satisfy himself into her unyielding body.

Just as he had done last night. This was normal for Danni Jones.

After her whirlwind marriage to this 'respected' property developer, life was initially good. Flush with money Liam and Danni lived in a fine prestigious house. She had independence, expensive clothes and with a few social events to attend to, she was never alone.

Oh, but she was.

Although she had her mother who lived in the next street and a couple of close friends with whom she met for lunch dates, within these walls she was abandoned. Her husband hardly uttered a word to her, but when he did, it was to criticise or to belittle. He had a talent for that. Making her feel worthless and inferior was his forte.

Her life was a farce, a charade. Many a day she would stroll out of her lovely home to visit her mother or to attend a bridge lesson, her smile would indeed be sincere as she greeted those she met.

But her heart was dead. Liam had crushed and abused it. Her heartbeat was merely a metronome, keeping in time with her empty painful existence.

Liam had begun to change after the first year of their marriage. Their physical relationship was increasingly one sided. Him needing more sexual gratification than that of a normal man, she in need to feel the tenderness of a loving touch. As a result due to the creeping unnatural sexual and violent demands from her husband, Danni would stay up late. Finally she would retire once he was asleep, sneaking into the guest room as he lay slumbering with a gut full of gin. But Liam would eventually find her and then abuse her.

As Danni lay in her lonely bed she recalled the day she discovered her husband was having an affair.

One evening she returned early from her Arts Club buffet, due to an increasing and persistent headache. Here she found her husband performing a crude and illegal sexual act on their neighbour's eighteen year old daughter.

Noticing that the young girl was enjoying such activities, and how enraged her husband would be at being discovered, she was reluctant to interrupt such a vile scene. Danni had quietly retreated, retracted her steps and silently ascended the staircase. Opening the elaborate doors, she flung herself onto the silky duvet and wept.

Reliving the nasty memory once more Danni could feel the wetness of her tears all around her. Dawn was breaking, the birds sang their innocent song to alert the world that a new and bright day was about to begin.

But today she didn't want a new day to start. Today her heart was filled with such sadness and despondency, Danni simply wanted it all to end.

Today she decided she would.

Sitting up she clutched her aching head, clumps of hair fell from her fingers as she swept stray locks from her pale face. He had been exceptionally rough this time. Her vagina stung with a vengeance as she started to edge her way off the bed. Looking back onto the bed she had indeed been bleeding, cerise fluid immersing with her sweat and tears, marbling the white bed sheets.

God, how she hated him.

With great effort she made her way to the bathroom. She needed to wash his stains off her raw tender body. After her shower, Danni reached into the bathroom cabinet. Shuffling through the mass of male beauty products, makeup and creams, she finally saw the Nitrazepam tablets. Staring into the bathroom mirror she saw her image for the final time. Her blonde hair was no longer matted with semen and blood; just smudgy tears stained her flushed complexion.

Danni's beautiful pixie featured face looked haunted. However a smile surfaced from her lips as she thought about the blissful death that awaited her and the revenge that would ruin her brutal husband forever.

***

The siren wailed as the ambulance approached the Jones's residence. Gillian sat on the bed sobbing inconsolably. Liam sat brooding on the wing backed chair staring at his wife's corpse. An empty bottle of pills and a half empty bottle of scotch lay next to her now peaceful body.

"What the hell has she done? I can't believe she would do this to me…to you Gillian. I can't fathom the reason why she would do such a thing."

Gillian raised her heavy head, eyes crystallising with fresh tears.

"Liam, I can't believe it. My baby. WHY?"

As Danni watched the pitiful scene before her, she did feel a deep sadness for her mother, but she also felt such elation watching the guilt, or was it anger that was shadowing her husband's handsome face.

Looking down at her own lifeless body for the last time, she travelled towards Liam, touching and sinking a part of her spirit into his tanned hand. He twitched, his arm waving spontaneously into the air.

"You are OK, Liam?" Gillian questioned, shocked at his sudden violent twitch.

"Yes, I just felt someone walk over my grave that's all." Gillian was not impressed with his tactless remark.

Yes, she could do it. Danni would find the right time to step into his body and make his life a living hell.

***

After two days of viewing the tragic yet false scenes of mourning that engulfed her home, Danni was resolute on her perfect plan of revenge.

Watching Liam throw himself into the arms of the young neighbour incensed her even more. She hovered over them as they indulged in sickening acts, feeling a strange notion of pity for the young slut, as she will soon have to succumb to his more violent demands.

As Liam and her mother sat together in the main bedroom discussing funeral procedures, Danni forced her plan into action. In spite of the limbo existence she had been experiencing for the last couple of days, this was the defining moment that she was waiting for.

"Yes, I loved her dearly Gillian, I don't know what I am going to do without her."

He sniffed, crocodile tears pricking into his eyes.

"She loved Delius…" he continued, "We can play her favourite music as her coffin arrives. You happy with that Gill?"

"Yes. Liam that would be fine. I know how hard this is for you, but we *all* are going to miss her so much. I really am shocked that she never even told me she was so troubled."

"I know Gill, if only she reached out..." Liam staggered his words laboriously; the grieving husband performance was of Oscar quality.

At these very words Danni *did* reach out. She once again approached her husband and held his shoulders firmly. Her stare bored into his cold calculating eyes.

He saw nothing, but he was about to feel a hell of a lot more. Sliding her essence into his, she began to mould and absorb herself into him.

Liam suddenly began to tremble.

"Liam, I know. Be strong. This is so hard for you..." Gillian got up from the bed to comfort her desperate son in law. Resting her hand onto his shoulder, he began to shake even harder. Standing back alarmed, Gillian felt a flurry of worry. Liam's eyes widened. His face turned into a sickening grey pallor. Gooseflesh dotted all over his quivering body, as if he had been pricked with invisible pins. Gillian watched as he fell to the floor. In great effort Liam eventually got to his feet, and then he finally screamed.

"*STOP!*"

Liam clutched his head as sweeping thoughts and images overwhelmed him. Sinking to the ground once more he cried out in a strangled voice, shaking uncontrollably. He began to rock from side to side; the images were too painful to endure.

"Liam! What's wrong! How can I help you?" Gillian now alarmed tried urgently to get a response, but Liam was oblivious to her words.

Rushing to the phone Gillian called the emergency services as Liam continued to writhe in torment. Gillian in a panicked voice stuttered the directions to a disembodied voice, tears staining her face as they slid down her foundation, streaking her face with pale uneven lines.

"...Yes, some kind of seizure I think, I am not sure, he is not aware of my presence."

Gillian placed the receiver after finalising the address and returned to the shaking distressed body of her son-in-law.

With a laboured effort, Liam got up. His eyes glazed robotically as he started to shuffle around the room. As a puppet awkwardly stomps across a cardboard stage, Liam staggered to the bathroom. Here he stared at his reflection. Gillian rushed in behind him.

"Liam, it's going to be fine, I have called for an ambulance and it's on the way."

Liam slowly turned to her and the faintest of smirks formed onto his lips. He didn't speak; he stood and stared at her blankly, as the corners of his month turned upwards.

Gillian now feeling uncontrollably nervous patted him on his cotton shirt and reassured him soothingly.

"Liam, don't worry, it's going to be just fine."

Picking up a cut glass that sat next to the wash basin, he suddenly threw it across the room, segments of glass splashing and crashing against the tiled floor. He picked up the largest jagged piece and turned it over in his hand. Examining it for what seemed like minutes, he finally held it still between his thumb and index finger.

Looking back into the mirror be began to cut his throat. Starting from behind his ear, sweeping down toward his Adam's apple he carved. Not satisfied with the results he began to tear and stab at his ashen face, starting with his eyes and mouth.

"Stop this now!" screamed Gillian as she tried desperately to grab the sharp shard of glass from his now bloodied hand. Succeeding miraculously, Gillian held the ugly serrated glass in her hand, and threw it to the floor. Liam stood silently in front of the mirror viewing his handiwork.

His face was torn. Exposed cheek muscle hung hideously from his split face, swinging loosely like a hanging piece of game.

Gillian screamed as she witnessed the gruesome self mutilation. She ran out of the bathroom unable to face the consequences of her son-in-laws actions any longer.

Her cries rung through the house as she exited the beautiful home, running to the nearest person who could eventually help her and the demented young man that continued to rip his own face to pieces.

Liam holding onto the wash basin with a tight grip began to bash his head into the mirror rhythmically, leaving chucks of fleshy matter dripping and slopping from the cracked surface, the open wound seeping with clots of skin and tissue. Suddenly he ceased his constant battering.

Staring at his face, he laughed. He laughed so hard, fresh spurts of coppery blood leaked from the gaping gash on his forehead. Not content with the state of his mangled face, he lurched out of the bedroom, down the sweeping staircase and eventually reached the kitchen. Blood oozed from every orifice of his face like a constant pouring tap.

The kitchen was immaculate but Liam's leaking presence was staining everything. He opened the cutlery drawer and grabbed a bread knife. Holding it close to his chest he awkwardly staggered to the lounge. Here he sat down on the love seat and put his head between his knees. Raising the knife high above his head, he began to saw away at the back of his neck. He worked slowly and delved deeply into the bone at the base of his neck. *Self decapitation was indeed a tricky task.*

Gurgling maniacal laughter echoed through the empty house as the blood flowed freely from Liam's open wounds.

It was time for the ultimate punishment. Death was too good for him. It would indeed be too final and a blessed relief for him. He must live. Live with these horrendous wounds and live in the fear and the guilt for the rest of his natural days.

The medics and Gillian finally found Liam unconscious but alive on the floor. Lying in his bodily detritus he moaned as Gillian gasped at the mess that surrounded her daughter's living room. Fresh tears of sadness and fear filled her eyes as she wished so much that her daughter was here just to comfort her, just to say, it's going to be alright.

As one of the medics lifted Liam's shattered body from the bloodied floor, from underneath his shirt Liam suddenly plunged the knife into the medic's groin, causing him to drop Liam heavily onto the floor. The medic screamed in agony as life drained from his body. The dying medic slumped onto the carpet as Gillian and his colleague watched in horror as the events unfolded in front of them so swiftly.

"Oh my God!" screamed Gillian, as the remaining medic desperately but fruitlessly tried to resuscitate his friend.

"He killed him!" Gillian continued to scream insanely, jumping up and down on the spot like an uncontrollable Jack in the Box.

Talking into his Walkie-Talkie, the medic held back tears as he called the police.

The man he was trying to save killed his dear friend; he was going down for life.

Liam was carried away on a stretcher as the medic was zipped up in the body bag. Unfair, but totally necessary. The sirens blared across the town, once again leaving the residence of Mr. Liam Jones.

***

Danni now free from Liam's polluted body, lingered in the blood soaked room, watching the police question her mother. She watched the forensic team carry out their job. She desperately wanted to comfort her mother; she had suffered enough, but she was strong. Even so, a tinge of guilt emerged from her soul. But this was definitely what Liam deserved. Jail was indeed the best place for him. Confined to a hospital for the criminally insane would be perfect.

This had been the most ideal acts of revenge. Relishing in her vengeance, she felt some solace at last. She had made him pay in the worst way possible.

For Danni now, it was time to find some level of peace herself. She needed closure. She needed to be at her final place of rest. But Danni would loiter and remain for a little while longer, to watch her husband's exquisite torturous days unravel before her.

PRAISE FOR CHARLOTTE EMMA GLEDSON

"Some authors tell stories we can believe in and follow as if they were real. When I read Charlotte Emma Gledson I am taken to a realistic world, with characters that I somehow know, even the weirder ones. Early on there is something sinister brewing, just below the surface of her prose. Then she goes for the jugular with a dramatic and horrible twist that takes your breath away in an instant. Her Stories are darkly surreal and brilliantly contrived.

In *The Lonely Tree* passion and dark revenge take on a whole new meaning, and will leave you with images you could not scrape from your mind's eye. In *Retribution* you feel the plight of a ghost, who suffered an abusive life, now free in the spirit world, haunting the halls of the one who mistreated her. The story takes you to a shocking twist that weaves yet again, and keeps you guessing right to the end. In *The Hand That Feeds* she knits a twisted dark tale that requires a certain taste, for blood." – **Matthew Pierce, author of *Reflected Evil* and *The Dark Curse Of Whispers***

"Charlotte Emma Gledson's stories are darkly poetic, edgy, and unsettling. Tales like *Retribution*, *Shadow Man*, and *The Lonely Tree* showcase just how diverse a writer she is. Remember her name because this new voice in horror is sure to be around for years to come." - **Alan Draven, editor of *Sinister Landscapes* and author of *Bitternest***

THE LONELY TREE AND OTHER TWISTED TALES OF TORMENT

"Charlotte Emma Gledson has a hauntingly beautiful and compelling way of weaving her short stories together. From her very first enticing sentence she garners the reader's complete attention as she lures you into her deliciously twisted world. A world where all fans of dark fiction need to visit." – **P. S. Gifford, author *of Curious Accounts of the Imaginary Friend***

"Charlotte Emma Gledson aims to terrify. She invites you into the heart of the monster, and shows you the suffering within the evil. This book will unleash a world of darkness...." – **L.B. Goddard , Author and Editor of *The Monsters Next Door Magazine.***

"Charlotte Emma Gledson has a taste for the macabre that is a rare quality among female writers...she embraces the descriptions of blood and internal organs with relish...a definite one to watch." – **Garry Charles, Award winning UK horror author and writer for *Gorezone* Magazine.**

"Charlotte Emma Gledson writes with the heart of a poet and the guts of a sniper. Her work is clever, keeping the reader entranced until that last moment when she delivers a twisted kick to the cherries. Definitely a new force in the horror world."- **Cassandra Lee, Author of *Darkness Springs***

ABOUT THE AUTHOR

Charlotte Emma Gledson currently resides in the coastal town of Gosport, UK. She shares her life with four gregarious children, her best friend, a scruffy mutt called Reg and a hoard of ventriloquist dummies and porcelain dolls. Her love for horror started at an early age, reading Stephen King, Richard Laymon and John Saul. Charlotte has a keen interest in Psychology and the workings of the criminal mind. She is a self confessed 'People Watcher'.

She and her twin sister were born in Preston, Lancashire. After spending a lot of her childhood moving from county to county, she keeps her roots for the Northwest and Cumbria close to her heart. The East Midlands, especially Southwell Minster also played a big part of her early life.

A classically trained singer, these days she happily maintains her vocal activities with karaoke and singing in the bath.

Since embarking on her writing venture, she has had numerous publications in anthologies and magazines, including Sinister Landscapes, the Gothic Anthology edited by Alan Draven, and the Ashen Eye Magazine.

She is currently penning her first supernatural/horror novel 'Bluebells For My Baby', due to be released December 2009.

Charlotte Emma Gledson can be found at:

www.charlottemmagledson.com

www.myspace.com/lotte38

www.ingramcontent.com/pod-product-compliance
Ingram Content Group UK Ltd.
Pitfield, Milton Keynes, MK11 3LW, UK
UKHW041437180426
11947UKWH00007B/489